KU-634-105

Books by Rick Riordan

The Percy Jackson series

PERCY JACKSON AND THE LIGHTNING THIEF*
PERCY JACKSON AND THE SEA OF MONSTERS*
PERCY JACKSON AND THE TITAN'S CURSE*
PERCY JACKSON AND THE BATTLE OF THE LABYRINTH
PERCY JACKSON AND THE LAST OLYMPIAN

THE DEMIGOD FILES
CAMP HALF-BLOOD CONFIDENTIAL

PERCY JACKSON AND THE GREEK GODS
PERCY JACKSON AND THE GREEK HEROES

The Heroes of Olympus series

THE LOST HERO*
THE SON OF NEPTUNE*
THE MARK OF ATHENA
THE HOUSE OF HADES
THE BLOOD OF OLYMPUS

THE DEMIGOD DIARIES

The Kane Chronicles series

THE RED PYRAMID*
THE THRONE OF FIRE
THE SERPENT'S SHADOW

The Percy Jackson and Kane Chronicles Adventures

DEMIGODS AND MAGICIANS: THE SON OF SOBEK,
THE STAFF OF SERAPIS & THE CROWN OF PTOLEMY

The Magnus Chase series

MAGNUS CHASE AND THE SWORD OF SUMMER

HOTEL VALHALLA: GUIDE TO THE NORSE WORLDS

The Trials of Apollo series

THE HIDDEN ORACLE
THE DARK PROPHECY

* *Also available as a graphic novel*

CAMP HALF≈BLOOD CONFIDENTIAL

RICK RIORDAN

PUFFIN

A special thank you to Stephanie True Peters
for her help with this book

PUFFIN BOOKS

UK | USA | Canada | Ireland | Australia
India | New Zealand | South Africa

Puffin Books is part of the Penguin Random House group of companies
whose addresses can be found at global.penguinrandomhouse.com.

www.penguin.co.uk www.puffin.co.uk www.ladybird.co.uk

First published in the USA by Disney • Hyperion, an imprint of Disney Book
Group, and in Great Britain by Puffin Books 2017

001

This book is set in New Baskerville/Fontspring

Printed in Great Britain by Clays Ltd, St Ives plc

A CIP catalogue record for this book is available from the British Library

ISBN: 978–0–141–37769–8

All correspondence to:
Puffin Books, Penguin Random House Children's
80 Strand, London WC2R 0RL

To all campers, past and present

CONTENTS

Movie Night 3
Three (Four?) Thousand Years and Counting 12
Creature Comforts 23
The Divine Cabins 29
The Big House 42
The Dining Pavilion 47
The Amphitheatre 50
The Camp Store 51
Magical Landmarks 57
The Grove of Dodona 61
The Cave of the Oracle 62
The Magical Border 69
Thalia's Pine and the Golden Fleece 71
The Athena Parthenos 79
Training Grounds 85
The Armoury 89
The Climbing Wall 90

The Combat Arena and the
Archery Range 91
The Volleyball Court 97
Tinkering 101
The Forge 102
The Arts and Crafts Centre 103
Bunker Nine 104
Wild Places 115
Grove of the Council of
Cloven Elders 120
The Pegasus Stables 128
The Myrmekes' Lair 129
The Geysers 131
The Strawberry Fields 133
Do I Get to Keep the T-shirt?
and other FAQs 140
Aw, Summer's Over 144
Map of Camp Half-Blood 148
About the Campers 150
Glossary 154

Praise me, demigods!

I made you this helpful film.

Trust me. It's awesome.

– Haiku by Apollo introducing his orientation film *Welcome to Camp Half-Blood*

Trust me. The film
was more awful than
awesome.
– P.J.

MOM[illegible]

H[illegible] everybody. Here[illegible] [illegible] as the [illegible] [illegible]

[illegible] have found [illegible]

[illegible] read [illegible] [illegible] and a few special [illegible] and [illegible] Elizabeth [illegible]

[illegible] too obvious [illegible] [illegible] topic.

[illegible] good. Thank[illegible] [illegible] with your [illegible] [illegible] and [illegible] [illegible] your [illegible] [illegible] happening.

[illegible]

MOVIE NIGHT

by Percy Jackson

Hey, everybody. Percy Jackson here. You might know me as the guy who helped save the world from total destruction – twice, but who's counting? I like to think of myself as just another Greek demigod lucky enough to have found Camp Half-Blood.

If you can read this, then surprise! You're probably a demigod too. That's because only demigods – and a few special mortals, like my mom and Rachel Elizabeth Dare – can read what's actually written here. To everyone else, this book is called *The Complete History of Pavement* and it's about . . . well, that should be obvious. You can thank the Mist for that choice of topic.

So, demigod, chances are you're making your way to camp with your satyr guide. Or maybe you've already arrived and are reading this with the hope that it'll calm your nerves. I'd say there's a fifty–fifty chance of *that* happening.

But I'm getting off topic. (I do that. I have ADHD. Bet you know what that's like.) What I'm supposed to do is explain the story behind this book.

A few months ago, Chiron – he's the immortal centaur who's also our camp activities director – was called away to rescue two unclaimed demigods and their satyr guide. (The satyr had got himself into a sticky situation. It took him days to get his fur clean.) Anyway, Argus, our resident security guard and part-time chauffeur, drove Chiron on this mission because, well, can you imagine a centaur driving an SUV? (You can? Hmm. Maybe you're a child of Hypnos and saw it in a dream.) Our camp director, Mr D (aka Dionysus, the god of wine), was MIA, so that left us demigods on our own.

'Don't destroy Half-Blood while we're gone,' was Chiron's parting instruction. Argus pointed two fingers at his eyes and then at us. This took a few minutes since he has one hundred eyes, but we got the message – be good, or else.

We went about our usual routines – combat practice, volleyball practice, archery practice, strawberry-picking practice (don't ask), lava-wall-climbing practice . . . You'll find we practise a lot here. We would have spent the evening in the usual way, too, with a campfire sing-along, if not for an offhand comment Nico di Angelo dropped at dinner.

We were talking about what changes each of us would make if we ran the camp, and Nico said:

'First thing I'd do is make sure the poor newbie demigods don't have to suffer through the orientation film.'

All conversation stopped. 'What orientation film?' Will Solace asked.

Nico looked puzzled. 'You know . . .' He glanced side to side, clearly uncomfortable with everybody watching him. Finally he cleared his throat and sang in a warbly voice to the tune of 'The Hokey Cokey': 'It lets the demigods in! It shuts the monsters out! It keeps the half-bloods safe, but turns mortals all about! It's Misty, and it's magic, and it makes me want to shout: the border is all about!' He punctuated the last line of the song with some half-hearted claps.

We stared at him in stunned silence.

'Nico.' Will patted his boyfriend's arm. 'You're scaring the other campers.'

'More than usual,' Julia Feingold muttered under her breath.

'Oh, come on,' Nico protested. 'You've all heard that annoying song, right? It's from *Welcome to Camp Half-Blood*.'

Nobody responded.

'The orientation film,' Nico added.

We shared a group shrug.

Nico groaned. 'You mean I just sang in public and . . . I'm the only one who's ever seen that stupid film?'

'So far, anyway,' said Connor Stoll. He leaned forward, a mischievous glint in his eyes. 'Where, exactly, did you see this cinematic masterpiece?'

'Chiron's office in the Big House,' Nico replied.

Connor pushed back from the table and stood up.

'Where are you going?' Will asked.

'Chiron's office in the Big House.'

Annabeth Chase – my awesome girlfriend, a daughter of Athena – frowned suspiciously. 'Connor . . . Chiron's office is locked.'

'Is it?' Connor laced his fingers together and cracked his knuckles. 'We'll see about that.' He turned to Harley, the oddly muscular eight-year-old son of Hephaestus. 'Want to come with? I might need help with the projector.'

'A projectile! Yes!' Harley pumped his fist.

'A projec*tor*,' Connor corrected. 'And you can't make it do anything but show the movie. No exploding upgrades. No turning it into a killer robot.'

'Aww . . .' Harley scowled in disappointment, but he followed Connor to the Big House.

I glanced at Nico. 'Now look what you've started.'

He snorted. 'This is *my* fault? What do you want me to do – stop them?'

'Stop them?' I grinned. 'Nah, man. I think we should get some popcorn ready.'

An hour later, we gathered in the amphitheatre to watch *Welcome to Camp Half-Blood*. Connor and Harley had successfully set up the screen and projector without any killer-robot-exploding mishaps, which I appreciated. I figured the movie would be a typical orientation flick – a monotone voiceover; a tour of the campgrounds; happy demigods going about their business, trying to pretend the cameras didn't exist. Then the opening credits rolled.

'Uh-oh,' Will muttered. 'This is going to be . . . interesting.'

It turned out the creative genius behind the movie was Will's dad – the god Apollo, which meant this was *not* going to be a typical orientation flick. No, as we soon found out, Apollo had written, directed, produced, hosted and starred in . . . *a variety show.*

For those of you who don't know what a variety show is, imagine a talent show on steroids, complete with canned laughter, pre-recorded applause and an extra-large helping of hokeyness. For the next hour, we cringe-watched as Apollo and our demigod predecessors performed in song-and-dance numbers, recited poetry, acted in comedy sketches and harmonized in a musical group called the Lyre Choir. Naturally, Apollo featured prominently in most of the acts. The one of him hula-hooping shirtless while satyrs capered around with long rainbow ribbons on sticks . . . you can't unsee that kind of thing. I'm seriously considering asking Hera to purge it from my memory.

(Okay, not really. I am not going through *that* again.)

Still, I get what Apollo was going for. Each number highlighted something important about Camp Half-Blood – the cabins, the training arenas, the Big House, et cetera, et cetera. The trouble is, Apollo didn't seem to know much about the camp. According to Valentina Diaz's assessment of the hair-styles and fashions, the movie dated from the 1950s, so maybe the film accurately depicted what Camp

Half-Blood was like back then. If so, yikes. Take it from me: a *lot* has changed in sixty years.

That's where *Camp Half-Blood Confidential* comes in. After seeing Apollo's film, we decided we *really* had to take action. We needed to offer our incoming demigods something better for orientation. And so – *BOOM*. You hold in your hands the definitive guide to life here at our beloved Greek demigod training facility. It's written for demigods by demigods, which means you get the inside, behind-the-scenes scoop on just about everything. You'll get the lay of the land, too, thanks to descriptions of sites written by Pete, a geyser god with a flair for selling it like it is. Oh, the stories we'll tell and the secrets you'll learn . . . though I promise you, I will *not* sing and dance with a hula-hoop.

One last thing: we wouldn't dream of completely depriving you of the *Welcome to Camp Half-Blood* movie experience. So we've included some choice excerpts from the film throughout the book – annotated by yours truly. Enjoy the show! (Cue maniacal laughter.)

Scene: Darkness. Suddenly, a single spotlight illuminates Apollo standing on the front porch of the Big House. The house is a bold red colour, a stark contrast to the short white chiton Apollo wears. He clears his throat and speaks.

Apollo: A poem by Apollo, recited dramatically by . . . Apollo:

O Immortal Chiron,
Centaur wise and true,
Trainer of our heroes,
Just remember who taught you.

– The opening scene of *Welcome to Camp Half-Blood*

Apollo's chiton was so short, I held my breath throughout this scene, praying he didn't bend over.
– P.J.

THREE (FOUR?) THOUSAND YEARS AND COUNTING

by Chiron

I was just a young centaur, living alone in a cave on Mount Pelion, when I first met Lord Apollo. He literally dropped in out of the sky, which nearly gave me a heart attack. It wasn't every day an A-list divinity with perfect teeth and glowing golden robes appeared on my hillside.

'You're Kronos's son, right?' Apollo pulled up a boulder and sat down. 'My dad is Zeus! He's Kronos's son too. So I guess that makes you my uncle. How weird is that?'

'Ah . . . yes, Lord Apollo.' I tried to control the twitching in my withers. 'Very weird indeed.' I noticed the sky was darkening even though it was only noon. 'Not to be critical, O Great One, but shouldn't you be driving the sun chariot right now?'

He shrugged. 'Actually, I parked it for a few minutes because Artemis is up there doing her lunar-eclipse thing.' He scratched his fashionably stubbled chin. 'Or is it solar? I can never keep them straight.' Suddenly he jumped from his boulder as if he'd had a marvellous idea. 'But that's not important! I remember what I came down here to ask you. I've never ridden a centaur before. Mind taking me for a spin around the block?'

'Um . . .'

He put his fingers to his temples and intoned, 'I predict you're going to say yes.'

FYI, centaurs hate being taken for a ride, either literally or metaphorically. Nevertheless, I managed a forced smile. 'I would be . . . delighted. Yes.'

'Oh, yeah!' Apollo crowed triumphantly. 'Who has two thumbs and the gift of prophecy?' He jerked his thumbs at himself. 'This god!'

As it turned out, giving Apollo a centaur-back ride was the smartest thing I ever did. Unlike others of my kind, I didn't belong to a specific tribe. I was a loner . . . and, sometimes, lonely. We bonded during that ride. I found that Apollo could be quite charming one-on-one, when he wasn't trying to impress his adoring throngs of fans. When we got back to the cave, he said something that changed my life.

'Uncle Chiron, I've decided to teach you some stuff.'

Perhaps he found the idea amusing: a nephew

teaching his uncle. Or maybe, being the god of prophecy, he suspected I had an important role to play in the future of Olympus. Whatever the reason, he chose to share his knowledge with me.

At first, he showed me simple things, like how to nock an arrow – 'Aim the pointy end *away* from your body' – and how to bandage a gushing battle wound. He taught me to make a lyre, play a number of hits like 'Stairway to Olympus' and 'Burnt-Offering Smoke on the Water', and even compose my own lyrics. Once, in an effort to refine my poetry skills, he sent me on a quest to find a rhyme for *arugula* so that he could finish an ode to a mixed-green salad. The best I could do was *pergola.* Apollo called my effort an 'ode fail' – the ancient precursor to today's 'epic fail' – but he continued to work with me.

The lessons went on for a year. Then one day Apollo showed up at the doorway of my cave with half a dozen young demigods. 'You know all that stuff I taught you?' he asked me. 'It's time to pay it forward! I'd like you to meet Achilles, Aeneas, Jason, Atalanta, Asclepius and Percy –'

'It's Perseus, sir,' said one of the young men.

'Whatever!' Apollo grinned with delight. 'Chiron,

teach them everything I showed you. Y'all have fun!' Then he vanished.

I turned to the youngsters. They frowned at me. The one named Achilles drew his sword.

'Apollo expects us to learn from a centaur?' he demanded. 'Centaurs are wild barbarians, worse than the Trojans!'

'Hey, shut up,' said Aeneas.

'Gentlemen and lady,' I interceded. 'I assure you I am a different sort of centaur. Allow me to teach you, and I promise I will not make you participate in any crude centaur behaviour like butting heads to the death or wearing drink helmets.'

Atalanta looked a little disappointed. 'Butting heads to the death sounds fun . . . but I guess I can give your teachings a try.'

We got down to business.

First, I assessed their combat skills. Aeneas performed surprisingly well for a son of Aphrodite; I expected him to be a lover, not a fighter, and yet he actually knew how to use his sword as a sword rather than as a fashion accessory. The other demigods had some work to do. Atalanta seemed to think all training matches had to be fought to the death.

She also referred to her classmates as *dirty, stupid men,* which made team-building difficult. Achilles spent his entire time in combat defending his right heel, an unusual manoeuvre that baffled me until I found out about his childhood dip in the River Styx. I tried to tell the boy to wear iron-shod boots rather than sandals, but he simply wouldn't listen. As for Asclepius, in one-on-one melees he had an off-putting habit of darting in and feeling his opponent's forehead for signs of fever.

Next I tested my pupils for ingenuity. I handed out random materials and instructed them to improvise potentially lifesaving objects. 'This ancient skill is known as *MacGyvering*,' I told them. Sadly, none of my inaugural group of students was a child of Hephaestus, so no one did very well with this assignment. When I hinted to Perseus that he could hammer and polish his Celestial bronze to make a mirrored shield, he rolled his eyes and scoffed, 'What would I ever use *that* for?'

Likewise, most failed miserably with musical composition. Only Jason came up with something memorable: a mesmerizing *stomp-stomp CLAP* rhythm that so stirred the blood we adopted it as our prebattle beat. (You can still hear that *stomp-stomp*

CLAP rhythm pounded out at athletic competitions today, along with the chant 'We will, we will . . . ROCK YOU!')

It was clear that the demigods had a lot to learn. But I didn't mind. As we sang together by the campfire that first night, I felt as if I finally had a tribe of my own.

I taught the six demigods everything I knew. Then I sent them out into the world, where they fulfilled their destinies as heroes. Triple-threat Atalanta earned fame as a fleet-footed sprinter, a sure-shot huntress and the only female Argonaut. Jason and his crew sailed into legend by securing the Golden Fleece and impressing the populace with myriad seafaring adventures. Achilles and Aeneas became mighty warriors – though, sadly, they fought on opposite sides in the Trojan War. (Spoiler alert: Achilles and Greece won, but Achilles was killed when he forgot to defend his heel.) Perseus discovered that a mirrored shield was useful after all when he faced a certain snake-headed gorgon, and as for Asclepius he became the greatest medical mind in ancient history. Their heroic deeds live on in the memories of mortals to this day.

So I must have done something right.

More demigods regularly arrived at Mount Pelion, and I trained them all. Word of my success spread. When my cave was no longer large enough, I built a one-of-a-kind full-immersion training facility in the foothills of Mount Olympus. I named it Camp Half-Blood because it was dedicated to training the half-divine children of mortals and deities. I also opened the doors to many other species, such as satyrs, pegasi and harpies.

The satyrs arrived en masse with this note from Apollo:

> I predict that in the future demigods won't be able to find Camp Half-Blood on their own. The world will simply be too large, too populous and too dangerous. When that time comes, send satyrs to track down your prospective students. Satyrs can find anything. They recently located a herd of cattle Hermes stole from me that even I couldn't find. Trust me: you need seekers, and they're the goats for the job.

The first Camp Half-Blood was modest – just an open-air arena for combat practice, a courtyard for meetings and dining, and a large stone building with sleeping quarters. The building made an impression on at least one camper, who exclaimed, 'Now *that's* a big house!' when she saw it. The name stuck, and forever after our headquarters has been called the Big House.

The demigods lived together in the Big House at first, but with more campers coming each year space became tight. Fights broke out. Demigods, it seemed, inherited rivalries as well as gifts from their godly parents. To keep the peace, I divided them into family groups and told them to design and build cabins that honoured their godly parents. Thankfully, the bickering died down to a quiet roar after that.

As Apollo had once turned over teaching duties to me, I turned over some of the training to experienced campers. I meant for them to pass along their knowledge of fighting and survival skills. And they did, but they also passed along family feuds, closely guarded secrets and hazing traditions. When the Hephaestus cabin almost burned down the dryads' forest during a late-night game of truth or dare ('Dare: blow up this amphora'), I asked Argus the Hundred-Eyed to join our staff as security guard.

At the time, Argus was recovering from a near-death experience. On Hera's orders, Hermes had brained him with a rock while Argus was guarding a white heifer – who was actually Io, Zeus's latest, er, lady friend. Hera saved Argus by turning him into a peacock. He eventually morphed back into his original form and jumped at the chance to come to Camp Half-Blood. Good thing he did, too, for without him, we might not have detected the first major threat to our existence: a monstrous horde that almost wiped Camp Half-Blood off the map.

'Whole bunch coming,' Argus reported late one night. 'Nasty ones.' (Even back then, he didn't waste words. Having an eye in the middle of your tongue makes talking uncomfortable, not to mention eating hot soup.)

We'd had random monster attacks before. We'd always fended them off. But this attack was different. It was an organized effort – I never discovered who organized it, though I have my suspicions – and it was *huge.*

Hundreds of monsters – nasty ones indeed – swarmed the camp from every corner. I sounded the conch horn to raise the alarm, grabbed my bow and quiver, and galloped into the courtyard. 'This is not a drill, people!' I cried. Demigods surged out of their cabins to face the greatest challenge of their young lives. Win, and Camp Half-Blood would endure. Lose, and the camp, along with countless lives, would be lost forever.

Fighting raged through the night. The demigods battled bravely and with skill, destroying monsters with swords, spears, arrows and other weapons. But we were far outnumbered. I feared Camp Half-Blood was doomed.

Then, just as rosy-fingered dawn peeked over the horizon, a new battle cry sounded in the distance. Former campers who had learned of our desperate plight now came charging to our aid. As one, we attacked our enemies with renewed vigour. We cut down one monster after another until their dusty remains blanketed the ground. Those we didn't send to Tartarus fled back into the wilds.

I had never been prouder of my campers, old and new. Nor had I ever been more ashamed of myself.

You see, I knew that so many demigods living in one place was like an all-you-can-kill buffet for monsters. Yet I had convinced myself that our campers needed no other protection than the skills we taught them. My pride had nearly been our destruction, but I learned my lesson. I immediately sent an Iris-message to Olympus asking for help. The gods heard our plea. The next day, a magical border settled over and around the grounds – a barrier that would both conceal the camp from unfriendly eyes and repel future attacks.

The camp has changed locations over the millennia, always grounding itself near the seat of Olympus as the gods move from one dominant nation to another. Thousands of demigods have called Camp Half-Blood home since that long-ago battle. You might know some of their names: Arthur. Merlin. Guinevere. Charlemagne. Joan of Arc. Napoleon. George Washington. Harriet Tubman. Madame Curie. Frank Lloyd Wright. Amelia Earhart. And many more demigods, still living, who have asked that I not reveal their identities. New names are added to the list each summer, and more still will join the ranks in the centuries ahead.

That is my hope, at least. For the demigods of the past, present and future are more than just campers to me. They make my immortal life worth living. They are my tribe.

Creature Comforts

SCENE: A background choir of demigod a cappella singers stands on stage. They're dressed in classic 1950s doo-wop attire – black suits, white shirts, skinny ties. Apollo, similarly attired except that his tie is gold, takes centre stage. He faces the singers and strums a chord on his lyre. He points to the boys.

BOYS [singing]**:** *Dooooooooo!*
[Apollo points to the girls]
GIRLS [harmonizing]**:** *Waaaaaaaaaa!*
[Apollo points to himself]
APOLLO [spit-singing]**:** *Pppppppp!*
[Apollo waves his arm]
ALL: *Dooo-waaapppp!*
APOLLO: Ladies and gentlemen . . . the Lyre Choir!
[Applause]
BOYS and GIRLS [singing soft background harmony with a slow beat]**:** *Doo-da-doo, waa, waa. Doo-da-doo, waa, waa.* [continues]
APOLLO [crooning to the beat]**:** *Marble may be marble-lous,*
And wood might be good.
Stone's a sturdy choice

For this half-blood neighbourhood.
But for my children's cabin,
I demand something more divine.
So give me precious metal,
[background harmony swells]
And make it GOLD every time!
ALL: *Gold, gold, gold, gold – there's nothing quite so bright!*
Gold, gold, gold, gold – it reflects Apollo's might!
[Apollo cuts off background singers]
APOLLO [crooning solo]**:** *Silver suits my sister*
But unattended it can tarnish.
Roofs of thatch are fine, I guess,
But why not add some varnish?
[background harmony resumes softly]
Vines of wine are creepy,
And abalone smells of fish.
[background harmony grows louder]
Red's too strong a colour,
And grey is boring-ish.
[background harmony grows louder still]
That's why my children's cabin
Is made of something more divine.
I'm worth that precious metal –
[background harmony swells]

So make it GOLD every time!

[Cheers and applause]

ALL: *Gold, gold, gold, gold . . .*

For the record, my
cabin's abalone walls
do NOT smell of fish.
- P.J.

JUNE

THE DIVINE CABINS

Brought to you by Pete the Palikos

Talk about kerb appeal! Tastefully decorated inside and out, these charming units are big on comfort and totally unique in style – one might even say each has its own personality! Of course, location is key, and you couldn't ask for a better spot than this. The twenty cabins are within easy walking distance of all camp amenities as well as training and recreational facilities. Don't see a unit dedicated to your particular godly parent? No worries! Once you're claimed, one can be built to suit. In the meantime, pull up a bunk in Cabin Eleven and stay awhile!

WARNING! The divine cabins area is an active construction site, so please watch out for exposed nails, exploding blocks and cracks that could plummet you to the Underworld.

SPACE COULD BE AN ISSUE

by Annabeth Chase

For generations, Camp Half-Blood had only twelve cabins – one for each major Olympian deity. The odd-numbered cabins were dedicated to the Olympic gods, the even ones to the Olympic goddesses – except for Cabin Twelve, which Dionysus took over when Hestia gave him her seat on the Council of Olympus, but that's another story. Anyway, after the second Titan War, my kind-hearted boyfriend, Percy, made the Olympians promise that *all* demigods, not just the kids of the major twelve, would have cabins of their own.

Which is just like Percy: doing something impulsive and compassionate, and making my life difficult in the process. See, I'm the camp's resident architect, which meant that the task of designing all those new cabins fell to me.

Don't get me wrong. I supported Percy's plan one hundred percent. But after building units thirteen to sixteen – Hades, Iris, Hypnos and Nemesis – the cabin area started to look cramped. I met with Chiron to discuss the problem.

'Space,' I told him, 'could be an issue.'

'Any ideas?' Chiron asked.

I brainstormed aloud: 'We build upward, combine new cabins into one tall complex. Demigods associated with the earth on lower levels, with the sky on top.'

Chiron shook his head. 'Intriguing idea, but experience has shown me that demigods from different families don't cohabitate well.'

'Okay, scratch that.' I pointed at the nearby forest. 'What about tree houses? Enclosed platforms, elevated walkways, ladders, rope swings –'

Chiron cut me off. 'The dryads wouldn't go for it. And imagine what would happen if a demigod took to sleepwalking.'

'Caves?'

'Only one available, and Apollo has claimed it for his Oracle.'

'Houseboats?'

'Sleepwalking again, plus the naiads would nix it. Also, we need the lake for trireme practice.'

I cast around for inspiration. My eyes fixed on Hestia, who was tending her hearth in the centre of the commons. You'd think a major Olympian goddess would attract a lot of notice sitting in the middle of camp, but Hestia came and went without any fanfare, usually in the shape of a young girl in plain brown robes. I hadn't noticed her, because she was so small and low profile.

Small and low profile.

An idea hit me like a Zeus-thrown thunderbolt.

'I'll get back to you tomorrow,' I told Chiron.

The old centaur chuckled. 'I know that look. You have an idea.'

'Yeah,' I admitted. In fact, my brain was buzzing. 'But I want to work out some details before I share it with you. See you at breakfast.'

That night I worked into the wee hours, pausing only to . . . well, to wee. In the morning I had my blueprints ready, but I still needed more time.

At breakfast, I broke the news to Chiron. 'I want to set up a construction site in the southern woods.'

He furrowed his bushy eyebrows. 'You're not thinking of building the cabins there, are you? As I said, the dryads won't –'

'I just need a secluded work area,' I said. 'I won't build anything big or permanent in that space. Trust me on this, okay?'

Chiron stroked his beard. 'Well, you've never let me down before. And I do owe you for designing those centaur-size bathrooms for the Big House. Very well, Annabeth. You have my permission.'

The next days were a feverish blur of measuring, sawing and hammering. By week's end, I'd completed a full-scale model of my design, premounted on a wheeled platform for easy moving. I bribed my pegasus friends Blackjack and Porkpie with some doughnuts, and they agreed to haul my creation out of the woods and into the commons.

A few campers wandered over to see what I'd built. 'It's supercute!' gushed Lacy from the Aphrodite cabin. 'But what is it?'

'A portable storage shed,' Clarisse La Rue guessed, eyeing the wheels. 'Or a covered chariot. No, wait. It's a rapid-deployment outhouse.'

'None of the above,' I replied, slightly offended. 'I call it a tiny house. Check it out!'

I threw open the door and invited them in, a few at a time. The main sitting room was compact but perfectly livable. Two built-in cushioned benches along the walls doubled as beds. I lifted the cushions.

'And see? There's storage underneath the beds for your clothes, armour, weapons. It's even long enough for that electric spear of yours, Clarisse.'

'Uh-huh.'

Clarisse sounded unimpressed, but that didn't dampen my enthusiasm. I pointed to the narrow staircase against the back wall. 'Upstairs is a loft with two more twin beds. Or it could be used as a game room, meeting area, whatever. I made the ceiling extra high so headroom isn't an issue. Under the stairs is more built-in storage. But the best part is over here.'

I squeezed past them and rolled open a narrow pocket door in the corner. 'Ta-da!'

'So it *is* an outhouse,' Clarisse said.

'It's a private bathroom,' I corrected. 'Whoever lives here never has to use the common facilities again.' I smirked at her, remembering the drenching Percy had once given her by blowing up the camp toilets. 'You of all people should appreciate *that*.'

Clarisse reddened. 'I'm coming down with claustrophobia.' She shoved past me and out of the door.

I turned to Lacy. 'You see the potential here, right? Microhouses are the future. This is cutting-edge architecture!'

She looked at the whitewashed walls, taupe cushions and unadorned windows. 'Well, it's kind of . . . boring inside.'

'It's only the model,' I said defensively. 'Whoever lives here can decorate it however –'

A tap on the door interrupted me. Chiron poked his head in and frowned. 'I would come in for a tour, but, ah, I fear there is no room.'

'Good luck,' Lacy whispered to me. Then she slipped past Chiron and hurried away.

I got out of the way so Chiron could come in and clop around the tiny house. It was large enough to accommodate him, but just barely. The entire walk-through took him about three steps.

When he emerged again, he looked deep in thought.

'It's only the model,' I told him.

'Hmm?' He focused on me as if trying to process my words. Then he exhaled with relief. 'Oh, a *model*. I see. In that case . . . yes, this might work.' He scanned the cabin area as if calculating the acreage. 'We'll need about four, don't you think? Please proceed with construction.'

Designing and building one tiny house had been

fun. Constructing four? I was over the moon. 'I won't let you down, Chiron!'

Two weeks later, I let him down.

I had been working overtime to modify my original design. I widened the doorways for better access. I got some magical paint from the Hephaestus cabin so the exterior colour of each new minibuilding could be changed with just a touch, making each one unique. I applied everything I knew about extra-dimensional construction to create impossibly deep storage containers, a larger shower in the bathroom, and built-in furniture that could be moved, collapsed or reshaped as desired. With a snap of your fingers, you could turn the living area into a bedroom, or a gym, or a dining room, or a military command centre that even Clarisse would be proud of. I added a dozen pre-programmed interior-decorating schemes so Lacy could never accuse the space of being boring. When I finally rolled out the new cabins and proudly presented them to Chiron, I expected him to be pleased. Instead, he looked puzzled.

'Um . . . is this it?'

I frowned. 'You asked for four, right?'

'Four *cabins.* Not four *models.*'

My spirits deflated like a bunch of month-old party balloons.

'Oh, dear,' Chiron murmured when he saw my face. 'That model you showed me – that was the *full-size* cabin, wasn't it?'

I nodded. 'That was the whole point, wasn't it? Saving space? I – I thought smaller buildings . . .'

He kindly laid his hand on my shoulder. 'Annabeth, your work is exemplary. But, as lovely as these units are, I fear that the children of, ah, *lesser* deities – for lack of a better term – will not appreciate accommodations so much smaller than the other cabins.'

The flaw in my concept was so obvious, I couldn't believe I hadn't considered it. The whole point of Percy's plan was so our new recruits – and their godly parents – would feel included at camp – equal, not *lesser*. But they wouldn't see my tiny houses as fun minimalist living spaces. They'd see them as yet another snub from the more powerful deities and their kids. I was so embarrassed that I wanted to crawl under a rock.

'I'll get Harley to blow up the tiny houses,' I mumbled. 'He'll like that.' I turned to go, but Chiron stopped me.

'Wait a moment.' He studied the units. 'These have wheels.'

'Yeah. I mean, they don't *have* to have wheels, but I thought –'

'Perhaps I was too hasty,' Chiron said. 'Let me try something.'

He put his shoulder to the closest minicabin and pushed it towards the next one in line. Having the strength of a stallion, Chiron had no trouble moving the tiny houses around. A few more shoves and he had arranged the four units so they were back-to-back, two on either side. The slanted rooftops joined into one centreline peak. In short, the tiny houses looked as if they'd been designed to fit together as a single structure that was about the same size as the older cabins.

'You know,' Chiron said, 'I think this might work quite nicely for our newest pair of demigods.' He called across the commons, 'Holly! Laurel!'

Identical twin girls who had been arguing on the steps of Hermes cabin raced over, each trying to push the other out of the way so she could be first.

'What's up?' asked the one on the left.

'Contest?' the one on the right asked eagerly. 'World war?'

'Something even more exciting,' Chiron promised. 'Annabeth, I'd like you to meet Laurel and Holly Victor, recently claimed daughters of Nike, the goddess of victory. Laurel, Holly, this is Annabeth Chase, the most gifted architect at camp. She redesigned the palaces of Mount Olympus!'

The twins' eyes widened in amazement. I felt a little self-conscious with Chiron praising me. I was, in fact, the *only* architect at camp. But that bit about redesigning Mount Olympus – that was true. It was the centrepiece of my college-admissions portfolio.

'What you see in front of you,' Chiron continued, 'is Annabeth's latest triumph: completely customizable, modular cabins.'

Laurel edged towards the nearest tiny house. She peeked inside the door. 'It's small.'

'Ah, but it's not!' Chiron said. 'It's *private*. Each module is for a maximum of four people. How many do you have to live with right now in the Hermes cabin?'

'Like a thousand,' Holly grumbled. 'All losers, too.'

I didn't think the Hermes kids would appreciate that, but I understood what Chiron was trying to do.

I chimed in. 'These modules are *brand new.* The bathrooms are state-of-the-art.'

Laurel's eyes lit up. 'Bathrooms *in* the cabin?'

'Yep,' I said. 'The furniture is programmable. The exterior colours, the interior design – it can be changed to whatever you want.' I touched the nearest cabin, willing it to turn from dull red to bright silver.

'Whoa,' said Holly.

'But we can't give brand-new cabins like this to just anyone,' I said. 'Whoever gets these, everyone else in camp will be totally jealous. We need to find the absolute best campers –'

'Us,' Holly said. 'Obviously.'

'Me,' Laurel corrected her sister. 'With you a distant second.'

'So who wants to claim a bunk first?'

'Me!' the sisters yelled simultaneously. They charged to the same front door, growling as they tried to push each other out of the way. Then they split apart and made for different entrances.

Shouts rang out from inside the cabins.

'I'll get to my loft before you!' one sister cried.

'Ha! No chance, loser! I'm already halfway up!'

Chiron turned towards me and smiled. 'There we are. Modular units that can be rearranged and moved as desired! Each cluster can be as big or small as we need it to be. More campers can be fit into the same amount of space as a regular cabin, but with more privacy and better accommodations. Annabeth Chase, you are a genius!'

I listened to the sounds of pounding footsteps and triumphant crowing from the Victor sisters as they argued about whose module was the coolest.

'Thanks,' I told Chiron. 'Genius was exactly what I was going for.'

My tiny-house mash-up brought the cabin count to seventeen. Three more units – Hebe, Tyche and Hecate – were added afterwards, and construction crews are ready to build more. Space might still be an issue some day, depending on how many gods we end up needing to represent, but you know what? Not one person has complained about my tiny houses being too tiny. In fact, when I get out of college, I may go into business designing portable microhousing for demigods. It beats building rapid-response outhouses, at least.

THE BIG HOUSE

Brought to you by Pete the Palikos

This four-storey sky-blue Victorian is a bona fide gem. The vast veranda offers ample space for pinochle players and convalescents alike. The basement is currently set up for strawberry-jam storage, but can also be used to hide the occasional demigod driven insane by the Labyrinth. The ground-floor living quarters, camp infirmary and combination rec room / meeting room are wheelchair accessible, as is a specially designed bronze-lined office. The rooms of the top floors stand ready to welcome overnight guests, while the attic, now free of its resident desiccated mummy, provides the perfect catch-all for camper discards and memorabilia.

TONGS A LOT, DAD

by Connor Stoll

People think I'm a thief, a sneak, a pickpocket and a lock picker. They're right, of course, but c'mon – how else am I supposed to spend my time while waiting for a quest?

When my brother, Travis, was here (he's in college now), we explored every inch of camp except one area: the Big House attic. No way either of us was setting foot in there while that ol' leather-skinned hippie Oracle was propped in the corner.

But then Spooky gave up the spirit and crumbled to dust on the Big House front porch. We saw our chance and took it. While everyone else was waiting to see if Rachel, the new Oracle, would survive the spirit invasion (spoiler: she did), we made our move round to the back door of the Big House.

It was locked. (Ha!) One pick, three clicks and *BOOM*! – we were inside. Thanks to past reconnaissance missions, we knew the way up to the attic. We pulled down the stairs and stuck our heads through the trapdoor and into a thieves' paradise.

We ignored the junk, like that old three-legged

stool the mummy used to sit on. But other pieces seemed to scream *Pick me! Pick me!* as if itching to be freed from their dusty attic prison. That glittery crown on the mannequin in the far corner. That emerald-pommelled sword hanging on the wall. That *sweet* Elvis-style rhinestone cape, which for some reason was draped across the shoulders of a stuffed taxidermic grizzly bear.

Travis and I had planned to take our time and really search through the stuff. But then, for no apparent reason, this beam of golden light shot upward through the floor and engulfed the Oracle's old three-legged stool. The light shut off as quickly as it had appeared, and the stool was gone. I didn't know what had just happened. Maybe Apollo was teleporting the stool to its new owner. Maybe somebody was randomly blasting disintegrator rays in our direction. Hey, you never know what those Hephaestus kids will do. Anyway, it kind of freaked us out. We decided not to stick around, just in case that weird beam came back and zapped us away too. We grabbed the nearest things we could reach – a canvas sack for me, a small wooden box for Travis – and got out of that attic faster than you can say Hermes Express.

Back at our cabin, we chased the other demigods

outside and told them to go play in the woods or something (being co–head counsellors does have its privileges). Then we sat down to examine our take.

Travis opened the lid of his box. His eyes grew wide. 'Whoa. It's a mystical bag of winds.'

My pulse started to race. 'Like the thermos Dad gave Percy that time? I've always wanted one of those! Let me see!'

All slow and dramatic, he pulled out a flat pink rubber sack with a thin nozzle at one end. 'Behold!'

I smacked him on the arm. 'That's a whoopee cushion, you idiot.'

He burst out laughing. 'Yeah, but I had you there for a second. Okay, your turn.'

I rummaged in my bag and pulled out . . . a pair of barbecue tongs.

Travis snickered. 'What are you going to do with those? You can't even toast bread without burning it. Are those things Celestial bronze at least?'

'Dunno. But there's an inscription: "For plucking the Tartarus napkin from the fire."' I turned them over and read the other side. '"One use only."' I looked at Travis. 'What the gods does that mean?'

'Well, Connor,' my brother said, 'I believe it means that you only get to use them once.'

'Shut up.' I almost threw my new tongs at him, then thought better of it. For some reason, that 'Tartarus napkin' thing made me edgy. I decided to keep the tongs on me at all times – at least until I got my one use out of them.

Good thing I did, too, because later that summer, a napkin from Tartarus *did* appear in the dining pavilion fire. It's a long story, but if I hadn't had those tongs . . . well, I'm not sure I'd be writing this right now.

As for Travis, he loved his whoopee cushion so much he slept with it at night. At least, he claimed those sounds I heard were coming from the whoopee cushion. I kind of feel sorry for his college roommate.

THE DINING PAVILION

Brought to you by Pete the Palikos

With its Greek marble columns and unencumbered views of the sky above, this inviting seaside facility screams classical elegance. The oversize tables, each reserved for members of a specific cabin, can easily accommodate up to twenty campers. The white tablecloths, edged with purple, add a dash of distinction. The menu boasts every food imaginable, and dishes are served and cleared by the loveliest dryads in the forest. Just don't forget to start your meal with a burnt offering to the gods! Oh, and ignore that crack in the marble floor – it's from a slight mishap when zombies were accidentally summoned from the Underworld. Nothing to worry about!

DINING PAVILION ANNOUNCEMENTS

REMINDER:

Hecate head counsellor Lou Ellen Blackstone and Hermes head counsellors Travis and Connor Stoll will conduct cabin inspections this morning. Veteran campers, please assist your new cabinmates. As always, cleanest cabin wins first-shower privileges; filthiest cabin will clean the pegasus stables.

That is all.

UPDATE:

It has come to my attention that in the course of today's cabin inspections, several personal items went missing. Stoll brothers, please report to the Big House immediately.

That is all.

UPDATE:

You may recall that during today's cabin inspections, several personal items appeared to have gone missing. I say *appeared* because, in fact, Lou Ellen hid the items by manipulating the Mist. Please see her for further details concerning the eventual reappearance of your possessions. Hermes cabin, my apologies.

Hecate cabin, please report to the pegasus stables. Blackjack and Porkpie are waiting.

That is all.

THE AMPHITHEATRE

Brought to you by Pete the Palikos

Just a stone's throw from the divine cabins, the Big House and Half-Blood Hill, this gathering spot features rising tiers of stone bench seating that curve around the central stage. The benches are as comfortable as any mortal movie-theatre chair, and there's not a bad view in the house. So take a seat, bask in the glow of the campfire and add your voice to the joyful sing-along with such favourite hits as 'Grandma Was a Gorgon' and 'This Is Not Kumbaya; This Is Sparta!'

THE CAMP STORE

Brought to you by Pete the Palikos

Tragedy! You finally make it to camp alive – only to discover that you forgot your toothbrush! You could Iris-message your mortal parent for a new one. But do you really want to walk around with drakon breath until it arrives? Instead, hit the camp store! While you're there, be sure to check out the latest line of wind chimes – available in Celestial bronze, silver and seashell – perfect for interpreting the voices of prophecy-spouting trees! If hanging bling in branches isn't your thing, how about the new Mythomagic expansion pack, Dual Deity Duel? The cards feature holographic images that change the gods' aspects from Greek to Roman and back. He's Ares! No, he's Mars! No, he's Ares again! Hours of dizzying head-to-head play! From tees to totes, whatever your needs, the camp store is your perfect one-stop shop.

TAKING INVENTORY

by Valentina Diaz

OMG, I just about *died* when I saw Apollo's orientation film. Those cute boys with their shorty-short swimming trunks . . . um, yes, please!

As a daughter of Aphrodite, I'm always on the lookout for fresh 'old-is-new' fashion ideas. Seeing those 1950s retro styles reminded me of a locked chest marked VINTAGE CLOTHING that I'd spotted in the back of the camp store a couple of days before. I'd been meaning to check out that chest, but Connor would never let me behind the counter to rummage through it. He was *so* annoying. He didn't understand the concept of browsing, like, *at all*.

Inspired by the film, I decided to take matters into my own hands. (Despite the fact that I'd just had a manicure.) I thought I might find some ideas for a new clothing line inside that trunk, so off I went!

Once inside the shop, I smashed open the lock on the trunk (Connor wasn't around). I was afraid I might just find musty retro T-shirts, knee-high tube socks (shudder!), skinny ties and other stuff that dated back to the last century. But the clothing I found went way, *way* back; I'm talking, like, *millennia* back. Shows you what cedar lining and sachets of potpourri can do to keep clothes fresh, am I right?

The first thing that hit me about the vintage clothing was the colours. Red, yellow, green, blue, indigo: it was like Iris had thrown up on them – in, you know, a good way. I was stunned, because I'd always imagined the Ancient Greeks dressed in white. I mean, that's what the clothing on the marble statues looks like, right? Then I remembered something Chiron had told me one time: the statues used to be painted, and they're white now only because the paint's worn off. Looking at the clothes in the trunk, I realized the Ancient Greeks actually *had* worn colourful clothes. It made me proud of my ancestors.

I recognized the styles right away. On top were chitons – tunic-like thingies that were dress-length for women, thigh length for men, and (giggle) super-short for male athletes. Underneath were some himations, or cloaks, and a few peploses. A peplos is a big rectangle of fabric that could be turned into just about anything – kind of like those cute beach cover-ups that convert from shoulder wrap to halter-neck dress to sleeveless dress to wraparound skirt. (Perfect for the budget-conscious shopper, BTW.) There were so many garments, I was afraid I'd miss something, so I grabbed a bunch of clothes hangers and racked those bad boys up.

'Oh, yeah.' I ran my hand over the linen and wool. 'It's dress-up time.'

For the next hour, I tried on everything (except the *strophion* – it was too much like a tube top, which no girl should ever wear, in my opinion). I borrowed Ancient Greek-style jewellery and footwear from the store's many storage lockers to complete my outfits. I was just twisting up my hair in an elaborate braided do when I saw one last item in the bottom of the trunk – an item I was pretty sure hadn't been there when I looked before.

'Holy Aphrodite's girdle!' I yelped as I pulled out . . . Aphrodite's girdle.

My hands trembled. I knew all about this particular article of clothing, though I'd never seen it in person before. Aphrodite was *super* careful about when she wore it. Crafted for Mom by Hephaestus (when they were still on good speaking terms), the girdle was more like a fashionable belt – a finely wrought wide band of gold filigree (twenty carat, if I'm not mistaken) – infused with magic. Supposedly, anyone who saw Mom wearing it got whipped up in a frenzy of passion for her. Not that she needs any help in that department. I mean, everyone who sees her gets the hots for her.

As I held the magical belt, I couldn't help wondering if its power would work for me. I thought about taking it for a test drive around camp. I'd saunter past a certain Brazilian boy's cabin and pause long enough for him to take a gander . . .

Tempting, I thought. But no.

I tossed the girdle back in the trunk. Why? Because I'd heard tales of Hephaestus cursing the items he made. The girdle probably wasn't cursed, but I wasn't going to chance triggering some dormant spell. Besides, any magic item used by the gods could be too much for demigods to handle.

As far as I know, the girdle is still at the bottom of that trunk. I left everything the way I'd found it when I closed up the store. But it makes me wonder . . . what was Mom's girdle doing there? Will there be a time when I need to use it for some emergency?

For now, though, I'll have to rely on my own charms to make people fall in love with me. Fortunately, I take after my mom. I'm pretty good at whipping up passionate frenzies . . .

Magical Landmarks

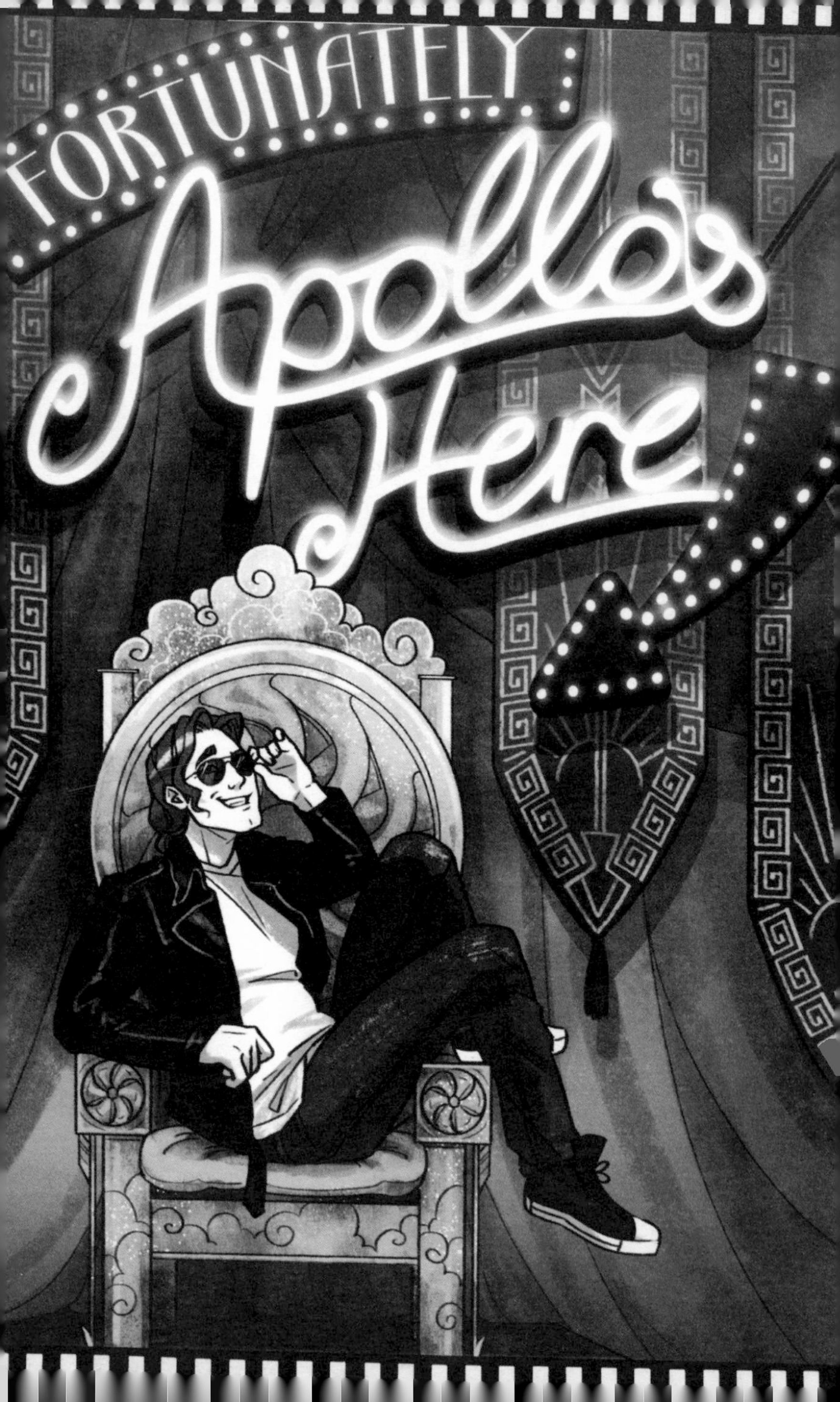
FORTUNATELY
Apollo's
Here

Scene: A room decorated with ornate tapestries, candles and carpets in hues of purple, red and gold. In the centre is a golden throne on a dais. Apollo, dressed in jeans, a brilliant white T-shirt, a leather jacket and sunglasses, lounges on the throne. On the wall is a neon sign that reads: FORTUNATELY APOLLO'S HERE!

Apollo: Next!

[A girl camper enters]

Girl: O Great Apollo, god of prophecy, tell me, will I ever find love?

Apollo: Find love? [mugs for the camera] I didn't know it was missing!

[Rim shot followed by canned laughter]

Apollo: Next!

[A boy camper enters]

Boy: O Great Apollo, god of prophecy, tell me, will I ever be rich?

Apollo: What's your name, child?

Boy: Albert, Great Apollo.

Apollo: Well, Albert Greatapollo, I foresee only one way for you to be rich . . .

Boy: What is it?

Apollo: [mugs for camera] Change your name to Richard.

[Rim shot followed by canned laughter]

Apollo: Next!

[A different boy camper enters]

Boy No. 2: O Great Apollo, god of prophecy, will I ever discover who my godly parent is?

Apollo: Dear child, the answer is right in front of you.

Boy No. 2 [looking around]**:** Really? Where?

Apollo: [stands up and spreads arms wide] Right in front of you.

Boy No. 2: I don't get it. Am I missing a clue?

Apollo: You're missing a clue all right. [mugs for the camera] One might even call you *clueless*!

[Rim shot followed by canned laughter and prerecorded applause]

– From the comedy skit 'Fortunately, Apollo's Here!' written by and starring Apollo

A comedy?
Really? Man, I'm glad I
didn't live through 1950s
television. . . .
– P.J.

THE GROVE OF DODONA

Brought to you by Pete the Palikos

Psst! Got wind chimes? Enjoy limericks? Want to know the future? Then hurry past Zephyros Creek and Zeus's Fist to the forest that holds this most ancient of all Oracles. Come on. It's not much further . . . Just follow the whispers . . .

THE CAVE OF THE ORACLE

Brought to you by Pete the Palikos

Yo, demigods! Are you craving a great new hangout? Word on the street is the Oracle's crib on Half-Blood Hill totally rocks. It's tricked out from top to bottom with purple curtains and massive sofas – with throw pillows for fresh pops of colour, yo! Check out the graphic wall murals, graffiti quotes and other funky artwork created by the one and only Delphic Oracle, Rachel Elizabeth Dare. You know what they say: if the torches are a-burnin', the prophecies are a-churnin'!

A CASE OF PPSS

by Rachel Elizabeth Dare

Do I scare you? I hope not. Most new campers think I'm über-spooky because I live part-time in a cave, have horrifying dreams about the end of the world, and spout enigmatic prophecies riddled with cheerful words such as *death*. Why anyone would find that disturbing is beyond me.

I delivered my first prophecy less than a minute after I accepted the spirit of Delphi. (If you want to know about the events triggered by *those* words, just ask any camper who lived through it. If you want to ask a camper who died through it, Nico di Angelo might set up a meet.) I thought I was prepared for the experience. I mean, I'd been channelling visions and seeing weird things most of my life. How different could mind-melding with an ancient spirit be?

Answer: very. Luckily, the god Apollo was on hand to help me to the Big House.

'You're experiencing PPSS,' he said as he led me up the stairs and to an empty hospital bed.

'PPSS? What's that?' I asked right before I threw up into a nearby bin.

'Post-prophetic stress syndrome. Just lie still. It'll pass.'

'You sure?'

He made a face. 'Hello? God of prophecy, remember?'

'About that,' I said. 'Why do you need an Oracle? Why don't you dole out your own prophecies?'

He looked skyward and rendered his reply in haiku:

'I'm a free spirit
Adrift in sunshine and song.
Office hours bore me.'

I thought about questioning whether *hours* was one syllable or two. But I let it slide, figuring he knew, seeing as he's the god of poetry.

Then I blurted out another question. 'Why can't the Oracle have a boyfriend?'

I'm not sure why I asked. I wasn't interested in anyone. (Well, not any more, anyway.) Guess I was just curious.

He didn't answer immediately. Instead, he broke off a leaf from a nearby laurel bough and crushed it between his finger and thumb. The air filled with its pungent aroma.

'Love can cloud the mind,' he said at last. 'An Oracle with an obstructed view is of no use.' His voice was sorrowful, and I remembered that he had once been madly in love with a nymph named Daphne who turned into a laurel tree to escape his amorous attentions. I guess he knew about clouded minds.

I changed the subject. 'Why do prophecies have to be so confusing? I mean, how come I can't just say straight up what's going to happen?'

He heaved a sigh, as if he'd answered the same question a million times before (which, given that he's immortal, maybe he had). 'That would be as much fun as a two-piece jigsaw puzzle. Mystery, intrigue, hints of danger, unusual rhymes – those are what makes a memorable prophecy! Take this one, for instance:

'Pinochle and ping-pong, ambrosia squares and
nectar,
An attic with an Oracle, a disembodied leopard,
A centaur in a wheelchair, a wine dude, serving time,
This omphalus of Half-Blood will welcome offspring
half-divine.'

Full disclosure: I had to look up *omphalus.* You hit the first syllable, by the way, like you would in *emphasis.* The word means *navel,* as in the centre point of something, not your belly button, though I suppose you could use it that way to impress your friends. *I might pierce my omphalus when I'm older.* Or mock your enemies. *You really don't know where your omphalus is? Ha-ha!*

But such navel contemplation came later. At that moment, Apollo was looking at me expectantly.

'Right,' I said. 'The prophecy describes Chiron, Dionysus and the Big House, obviously.'

'Obvious to you, sure,' Apollo agreed. 'But what if I told you that little prophetic nugget was delivered more than a thousand years ago?'

I had a sudden vision of people back then hearing the words *pinochle, ping-pong* and *dude.* Gods only knew what they thought they meant. Food? Weapons? Clothing? They wouldn't have had a clue. And what did Chiron make of the bit about the centaur in a wheelchair?

The truth struck me like a cold, wet cloth to the face. Unless they were immortal, the people who heard that prophecy died without understanding what it meant. They may have gone crazy or even perished on quests attempting to decipher its meaning.

The thought made me really sad, then super

anxious about prophecies I might utter some day. 'Apollo,' I whispered, 'will my words send people on hopeless quests?'

'Oh, Rachel.' Apollo patted my hand comfortingly. 'Yes.'

'Well, that's just peachy.' I didn't mean to sound bitter, but honestly I was starting to have significant second thoughts about the whole Oracle gig.

Apollo stood up then. 'You need sleep,' he said. 'But, before I go, I have something for you.' He pointed at the ceiling. A beam of golden light issued from his fingertip. A moment later, a present clumsily wrapped in gold foil paper thudded next to me. (I found out later that the beam of light almost gave the Stoll brothers heart attacks.) 'Open it.'

Inside was a rickety-looking three-legged stool. 'Um . . . thanks?' I said.

'It's the original,' he told me. 'From Delphi. Well, from the Big House attic, more recently, where it languished underneath the posterior of your predecessor for far too long.'

Understanding dawned on me. 'This is *the* tripod of Delphi. The one the first Oracle sat on thousands of years ago. You're giving it to me?'

'I could have let you try stealing it, I suppose,'

Apollo said, scratching his head, 'but that didn't go so well for Heracles when he tried it. He was punished with a year of women's work for his crime.'

I cocked an eyebrow. 'Excuse me? *Women's* work?'

Apollo waved dismissively. 'Housework, chores, whatever. All that mattered was that for a blowhard like Heracles, washing dishes and sweeping floors was a well-deserved punch in the ego.' He patted the stool lovingly. 'The butts of many powerful women have rested here.'

'I'm honoured to be adding my derriere to the list.' As the words came out of my mouth, I realized I meant it. For good or bad, I was the new Oracle of Delphi. I celebrated the momentous occasion by throwing up again.

Things have been a little quiet around my cave of late (unless you count my recent mural-eradicating, sofa-flipping, curtain-shredding tantrum, which I sincerely hope you won't). For some reason, the pilot light of prophecy has gone out, and Apollo hasn't been able to reignite it.

But don't worry. I predict I'll be spouting green smoke and confusion again by the time you're ready for a quest. And that will be soon, I have a feeling . . .

THE MAGICAL BORDER

Brought to you by Pete the Palikos

Tired of living with mortals who smell of BO, cigars and garlic? Then step through the border and leave the stench behind! Powered by the strongest Mist and guaranteed to repel even the most determined monsters* and nosiest mortals, this invisible barrier surrounds Camp Half-Blood with the best demigod protection magic can conjure. And that's not all! As an added bonus, inside the borders of camp, you'll be enveloped in delightful springtime weather all year round. So, if you're ready to say goodbye to stink, slush and certain death, come through the border today!

* Some restrictions apply. With invading armies and giant, hostile animated statues, results may vary.

THALIA'S PINE AND THE GOLDEN FLEECE*

Brought to you by Pete the Palikos

Created by Zeus himself to embody the life essence of his dying daughter, Thalia Grace, this storied tree marks the easternmost boundary of Camp Half-Blood. The pine flourished for five years, strengthening the border with its magic. Then Luke Castellan, foul minion of Kronos, poisoned it with elder python venom. The valiant tree clung to life until the Golden Fleece, that ancient mystical blanket shorn from a flying ram, restored its vigour. The Fleece's curative powers even released Thalia from her piney imprisonment – *sap-free*! Today the Golden Fleece and the Athena Parthenos energize the camp's protective barriers, but the pine tree remains as a tribute to Thalia Grace's bravery. It also smells really nice.

*Approach at your own risk. Peleus the guardian dragon only *appears* to be sleeping.

ON THE OUTSIDE LOOKING IN

A Conversation via Videoconference with Sally Jackson and Frederick Chase

by Thalia Grace and Leo Valdez

Thalia: Leo, did you get this stupid recording device working yet? What? I can't hear you! *What?* Gods, and people wonder why I joined Artem– Oh. Hi, everyone. Apparently, I'd muted Leo.

Leo: You'd be surprised how often people do that to me.

Thalia: Would I? So, we're talking with Sally Jackson, mother of Percy, and Frederick Chase, father of Annabeth, via a four-way videoconference set-up that Leo *vows* will work just fine.

Leo: Did I vow? Not on the River Styx. I know better!

Sally: Hello, Thalia, dear. You're looking particularly punk today. And Leo –

Leo: As smokin' hot as always, am I right?

Sally: Well, smoking, anyway. You're smouldering through your T-shirt.

Leo: Whoops. Let me put me out. There.

Thalia: *Anyway* . . . we're here to get insight into

how mortal parents feel about Camp Half-Blood. Ms Jackson, Dr Chase, you've never actually set foot in the camp, is that right?

Sally: That's correct. Even though I can see through the Mist better than most mortals, I can't get through the magic border. I suppose if someone gave me direct permission to enter, I might be able to, but even then I'm not sure. The closest I ever got was the summit of Half-Blood Hill, and honestly I'm not anxious to try that again.

Leo: Yeah, Peleus the dragon might snack on you. Or the Athena Parthenos might zap you with her laser-beam eyes. Wait . . . does the statue even have laser-beam eyes, or is that just my wishful thinking? Not that I'd want *you* to be zapped, Mrs J.

Sally: Thank you, dear, that's very comforting to know.

Thalia: How about you, Dr Chase?

Frederick [puts down model aeroplane he was tinkering with]**:** Hmm? Oh, yes. Camp. No, never been, though it would be fascinating to study from a historical point of view. From what Annabeth has told me, the only uninvited mortal to make it through unscathed was Rachel Dare.

Thalia: I heard there was this pizza guy once . . . but

that's probably just a camp legend. Ms Jackson, you may recall that I was there – in pine-tree mode – the first time Percy passed through. I don't remember it, though, because . . . well, I was a tree.

SALLY: I'm a little foggy on the details myself.

FREDERICK: Something about a Minotaur?

SALLY: *Everything* about a Minotaur.

THALIA: Can't say my first time at the border was much better. Fighting off monsters one minute, then – *ZAP!* – oozing tree sap the next.

FREDERICK: My word, Thalia, I just realized . . . I've never thanked you for saving Annabeth's life that day!

THALIA: It's ancient history, Dr Chase, no worries.

FREDERICK: Perhaps I could ship you this model of Amelia Earhart's 1921 Kinner Airster biplane that I just finished. It's a lovely replica!

THALIA: That's really not necessary. But tell me, both of you, now that things have settled down in the demigod world, wouldn't you ever want to see Camp Half-Blood for yourselves?

SALLY: Well . . . yes, of course, if there were no Minotaurs or, ah, laser-beam-shooting impediments. In fact, after Percy's first summer there, I *did* ask Chiron if he'd open the camp for just one day so families could visit. Mortal families, that is.

Leo: I'm guessing Chiron said no.

Sally: Yes.

Leo: Wait . . . he said yes?

Sally: No, he said no.

Leo: I'm confused.

Thalia: What else is new?

Sally: Chiron told me that he did have a visitors' day once, about a hundred years ago. But it did not go well.

Thalia: What happened?

Sally: Somehow an eidolon, a manticore and a disgruntled Party Pony found out about it. The eidolon possessed a camper's half sister, the centaur got his hands on a cap of invisibility, and the manticore disguised himself as a family dog. They infiltrated the camp.

Thalia: Not a bad plan, though I prefer a direct assault myself.

Sally: It might have worked, except the centaur wasn't the sharpest *kopis* in the drawer. He couldn't help showing off during the archery exhibition. Shot three bull's-eyes before someone noticed the bow was floating in mid-air.

Thalia: What about the manticore and the eidolon?

Sally: They caught the manticore spiking the

volleyballs. With its tail spikes, that is, not actually hitting the balls over the net.

Thalia: Volleyball existed a hundred years ago?

Frederick: Yes, indeed! Volleyball, or *mintonette* as it was originally called, was invented in 1895 by William G. Morgan in – Sorry. Once a professor, always a professor.

Sally: The eidolon caused the most destruction. It hurled a jar of Greek fire at the climbing wall, which then dripped with flames for hours afterwards. That's where Chiron came up with the idea of adding lava as a permanent feature for the wall, by the way.

Thalia: That Chiron. Always finding ways to turn death-defying challenges into much worse death-defying challenges. So what happened to the intruders?

Leo: Festus!

Frederick: Gesundheit.

Sally: I think he means Festus, his bronze dragon.

Leo: The one and only! You know he was originally built for border patrol, right? What I heard, he had a killer body back then. Like, literally – he had this spiky exterior plating so he could use his body to kill. Man, I bet he body-slammed that manticore right back to Tartarus!

Sally: Chiron did mention there had been some body-slamming. As for the eidolon, it took the combined powers of Aphrodite's children to charmspeak the spirit out of the girl.

Leo: And the centaur?

Sally: Chiron sorted out the cause of his fellow centaur's anger – something about not getting his fair share of root beer the last time he was at camp. Chiron, being kind-hearted, let him return to his tribe with a warning. But the camp hasn't held another visitors' day since.

Thalia: I guess I see why. And now that I think about it, a family day might be depressing for some of the campers who don't *have* family. I mean . . . who'd come visit me? Or Leo?

Leo: Speak for yourself, Tree Girl. I may not have much family, but all the ladies would flock to me like moths to my flame. Aw, yeah!

Thalia: Aw, *yech.*

Frederick: Now, now. We'd visit both of you! Er, that is, if you *do* schedule a visitors' day, and if I can remember to put the date on my calendar . . .

Sally: [coughs] I think the important thing is that I know Percy and the rest of you have a safe place to be. I don't feel a driving need to see the camp for myself. It's just comforting to know that when my son is there, he's with friends who have his back.

Leo: Also his front, his sides and his top. I draw the line at his bottom, though.

Sally: However, there is something I'd like to get on the record. Something I think all mortal parents would agree with.

Thalia: Sure, go ahead, Ms Jackson.

Sally: Demigods, we love you.

Frederick: Agreed.

Sally: But if you don't start Iris-messaging us a little more often, we're going to sic Coach Hedge on you. Take care of yourselves, and make us proud. You always do!

THE ATHENA PARTHENOS

Brought to you by Pete the Palikos

Recently recovered from a massive spiderweb deep within the bowels of Rome, this priceless forty-foot-tall chryselephantine* statue of the goddess Athena is accessorized with a sphinx-and-griffin crown, a handheld statue of the goddess Nike, a shield and a snake. It exudes its protective and somewhat fierce magic from its new home atop Half-Blood Hill.

*chryselephantine: sculpted of gold and ivory

A PEPLOS FOR ATHENA

by Malcolm Pace

Ask anyone here and they'll tell you I'm a level-headed guy. Big on logic, small on drama. A think-first, leap-second sort of demigod. Comes with being Athena's kid, I guess.

So I was a little freaked out when the visions started hitting me.

Demigods have nightmares regularly – as you'll find out soon enough, I'm afraid. But these visions would happen when I was awake. I'd be walking along, not a care in the world, when – *BAM*! My brain would be flooded with images of some Ancient Greek festival. I saw athletic events like in the Olympics, plus musical contests, poetry readings and even beauty pageants. I witnessed winners receiving amphorae of olive oil (super valuable back then). I watched a parade that ended with a life-size wooden statue of Athena being ceremoniously draped with a huge colourful cloth.

This mental slide show scrolled through my mind on four separate occasions. By the fourth rerun, I wanted answers. One, what the heck was this festival?

Two, where were the visions coming from? And three, why was I having them?

I got the answer to the first question by doing a little digging in our cabin's research library. Buried in one book was a description of a festival called the Great Panathenaia that was held every four years in Athens in honour of my mother. I learned that the wooden statue was the Athena Polias, meaning Athena 'of the city', and the cloth was a special peplos (a versatile garment that could be worn as a floor-length skirt, a top-and-skirt ensemble, a shawl, or – Gods, I sound like Valentina! Sorry!) woven with images depicting Athena's greatest triumphs, like the time she defeated the giant Enceladus.

So I'd been seeing the Great Panathenaia. Now I just had to figure out where the visions were coming from and why I was seeing them.

The 'where' proved surprisingly easy to solve. Every time the visions hit me, I was near Half-Blood Hill. Therefore, my logical brain told me, something in that area was causing the visions. Conclusion: the something was the Athena Parthenos.

If you don't believe that's possible, just go up to Half-Blood Hill and experience the Athena Parthenos's power for yourself. The statue radiates magic. Its eyes follow you. It's so lifelike, you expect it to speak. Trust me, once you feel its power, you'll understand why I decided the statue was channelling the pictures from the past into my head.

So that left the question of why. I explored several possibilities but kept coming back to one: Mom was giving me a not-so-subtle hint. I deduced she missed having a festival dedicated just to her. I further deduced she wanted me to resurrect that festival here at Camp Half-Blood. She would never come right out and tell me that, of course. Demanding to be honoured isn't her style. That's why she used the statue as a go-between.

Just to be sure I was right, though, I whispered my conclusions to the Athena Parthenos. Yes, I felt a little silly talking to a statue, and of course the statue didn't reply. Neither did Mom. Not directly, anyway. But that night an amphora of olive oil appeared beside my bunk. This either meant she was giving me a favorable omen or she wanted me to make a *whole lot* of pizza. I figured it was the former.

The next morning I told my siblings and Chiron everything. The Athena kids were all over remaking the festival. Chiron himself had attended the original

Panathenaia back in the day, so he readily green-lit the project.

Our inaugural Camp Half-Blood Panathenaia is scheduled for next August, to coincide with the dates of the original festival and Mom's 'sprang from Zeus's head' day. That gives us Athena kids about a year to construct a wooden Athena Polias statue, weave a ginormous peplos, organize the competitions and plan the procession. (Some of my siblings suggested just making a peplos for the Athena Parthenos, but firstly I don't think there's enough cloth on Long Island to make a serape that big, and secondly the Ancient Athenians didn't do it that way. They used a wooden statue made especially for the festival. I want to do it the traditional way because, well, this is all about bringing back a tradition.)

Am I worried we'll be ready in time? Nah. As children of Athena, planning and organizing runs in our blood. Plus, other campers are already volunteering to help. If you want to lend a hand, the sign-up sheet is on Cabin Six's door.

And Mom? I think she approves. The last time I was near the Athena Parthenos, I swear it winked.

Training Grounds

SCENE: Apollo jogs along the beachfront, shooting arrows backwards from his golden bow. He's followed by campers dressed in combat gear, jogging in military formation.

APOLLO: I don't know but I've been told!
CAMPERS: We don't know but we've been told!
APOLLO: The sun god's got a bow of gold!
CAMPERS: The sun god's got a bow of gold!
APOLLO: He's the best shot in the land!
CAMPERS: He's the best shot in the land!
APOLLO: Augh! [Apollo trips and lands on his backside] I've fallen in the sand!
CAMPERS [jogging circles around him]**:** Augh! He's fallen in the sand!
APOLLO: I meant to do that, so don't laugh!
CAMPERS: He meant to do that, so don't laugh!
APOLLO [tries to get up but falls back again]**:** Ow! I hurt my godly calf!
CAMPERS: Ow! He hurt his godly calf!
APOLLO [glowering and starting to glow]**:** If you want to live another day . . .
CAMPERS: If we want to live another day . . .

Apollo [radiating brighter]**:** STOP REPEATING WHAT I SAY!

Campers: STOP – um . . .

– Military cadence written, chanted and abruptly ended by Apollo

Best. Scene. Ever.
– P.J.

THE ARMOURY

Brought to you by Pete the Palikos

Centrally located and stocked to the rafters with spears, swords, daggers, shields, bows and arrows, and clubs, the armoury is a must-see for those in need of deadly weapons. Dig through, and you might even find one imbued with magical abilities. So don't delay – your stabber, slicer, slasher or basher awaits!

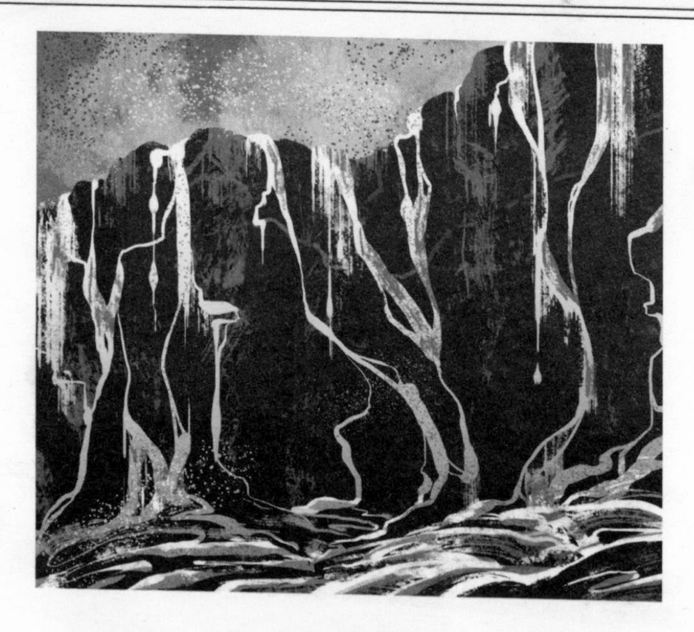

THE CLIMBING WALL

Brought to you by Pete the Palikos

Where is fun spelled *l-a-v-a*? The climbing wall, of course! Originally created to fine-tune reflexes and test hand–eye coordination, the climbing wall has become every camper's top spot for primal-screaming practice. If a fall from halfway up the side doesn't send you to the Big House infirmary, the slamming walls or molten magma will. So come on up – just don't look down!

THE COMBAT ARENA AND THE ARCHERY RANGE

Brought to you by Pete the Palikos

More demigod blood has been shed in this circular fighting zone than anywhere else in camp. So what are you waiting for? Strap on your armour and get ready to sweat, because you ain't *never* had a workout like this before! You'll engage every muscle as you slash with your sword, jab with your spear, smash with your shield and stab with your dagger. And that's just the warm-up! Now that your blood is pumping (inside your body, outside your body, whatever), it's time to test your metal against a straw dummy – or to test your *mettle* against a live opponent. But remember: the hits are real and so is the blood, so keep your guard up!

Striking from afar more your style? We've got you covered! Just a javelin's throw from the combat arena is the archery range, with its array of boldly coloured targets, their bull's-eyes daring you to hit them with a well-aimed arrow. Just be on the lookout for errant projectiles so you don't become a target yourself!

THE ARES PEACETIME CHALLENGE

by Ellis Wakefield

To be a great head counsellor, you have to be more than just the oldest sibling in a cabin. You have to be a leader – smart, strong, decisive, brave – and also a fearless fighter. Clarisse La Rue, our previous head counsellor, was all those things and more. Sherman Yang? Him, I wasn't so sure about.

Sherman took over when Clarisse left Camp Half-Blood to go to college. He was a typical Ares kid, meaning a ferocious muscle-bound fighting machine with a yen for bloody conflict and a disdain for peace. But, as impressive as those qualities were, I wondered if they were enough to lead our cabin. More importantly, were they enough to lead us to victory over the other cabins? If not . . . well, let's just say I was secretly studying him to find his Achilles' heel.

Not long after Sherman took over, Ares cabin scored poorly on the daily camp inspection. One of my sisters had left a plate of sticky, sweet barbecue under her bunk, and ants had swarmed it. Not the gigantic *myrmekes* – they prefer shiny things to smoked meats. It would have been okay if the myrmekes had invaded, actually. Things had been so calm lately, I wouldn't have minded going a few rounds with them, sword versus mandible.

Anyway, our chore that day was combat arena and archery range prep. I loved practising in the fighting zones, but tidying up afterwards and getting everything ready for the next session? I'd rather tackle the Nemean Lion and, from the looks on my cabinmates' faces, they felt the same way. We might have staged a sit-down if non-aggressive protest didn't sicken us so much.

Instead, we trudged out to the arenas. To my surprise, a number of campers from other cabins were there too. So was Sherman, which kind of surprised me, because he normally wasn't the first one on-site when we had to do chores.

'Ares cabin!' he barked. 'Take a knee!'

I didn't get what was going on. We were supposed to be doing prep. And why were all these other campers here? Nevertheless, we Ares kids knelt as one and waited to see what would happen.

'I'm running a friendly little relay race today,'

Sherman announced to the whole crowd. 'Who wants in?'

The Ares kids all started raising our hands, naturally. I still didn't understand why Sherman was holding a race instead of making us do our assigned tasks, but I wasn't going to argue.

He gestured at us impatiently. 'No, no, not you, Ares cabin. You're just here as observers. This race is in the arena and archery range, and you know those areas too well. It wouldn't be fair to the other competitors.'

Fair? How could *this* guy be the head of our cabin? I almost stormed away in disgust. But then I noticed the crafty twinkle in Sherman's eye. He was up to something. What, I didn't know. But I wanted to find out.

'What do we win?' asked Cecil Markowitz. That kid, always thinking about the potential payout.

Sherman smiled slyly. 'Whoever finishes first gets to fire the T-shirt gun tonight.'

His announcement caused a ripple of excitement. Guns weren't a big favourite at Camp Half-Blood; most campers preferred the traditional weapons of Ancient Greece. The Ares cabin T-shirt gun was one of the few exceptions. It shot tightly rolled Half-Blood tees fifty feet in the air. It was a real crowd-pleaser during camp sing-alongs and volleyball matches.

After some jostling and debate, five contestants stood up to volunteer: Will Solace, Miranda Gardiner, Billie Ng, Cecil Markowitz and Damien White. My money was on Will or Damien to win whatever Sherman had cooked up. Will, because he was clever and quick. Damien, because he was devious.

'Competitors!' Sherman held up a hand, fingers splayed. 'This race consists of five tasks, which are as follows: each of you must sharpen the blades of two practice swords. Then you must replace four used archery targets with new ones. After that, you polish a shield. Then you must replace the points on three spears. Finally, reattach a straw dummy's limbs and head. Then return here to me.' Sherman curled his fingers into a fist. 'Any questions?'

I was biting the inside of my cheek to keep the smirk off my face. I had to give it to Sherman – he'd come up with a great plan to get the other campers to do our work. Nothing like the promise of firing a large gun to keep people from thinking straight.

Sherman lined up the racers and bellowed, 'Go!'

Off they raced. Twenty minutes later, Miranda crossed the finish line first. Gasping, she raised a triumphant fist in the air. Sherman grabbed her in a hug, then quickly let go, red-faced and grinning sheepishly. We Ares kids cheered lustily for the victor, for the chores we didn't have to do, and most of all for Sherman – our ace head counsellor.

THE VOLLEYBALL COURT

Brought to you by Pete the Palikos

Whether you're a serious player or just a camper looking for a little fun competish, there's no better place than the volleyball court to feel the sun on your back, the wind in your hair, or a ball in your face. Come to play, come to watch, come to catch a T-shirt from the Ares cabin's gun – just come!

GAME CHANGER

by Laurel and Holly Victor

LAUREL: Check it – we're in charge of the volleyball court.

HOLLY: We keep it ready to go.

LAUREL: Makes me sick.

HOLLY: The court?

LAUREL: No, that campers play for fun, as in –

HOLLY: Don't say it!

LAUREL: – *recreationally.*

HOLLY: Gross! Pointless!

LAUREL: Totally goes against our heritage.

HOLLY: True that. Ancient Greeks loved organized competitive sports.

LAUREL: Hello, ever hear of the Olympics?

HOLLY: Or the Panathenaia?

LAUREL: Sand courts were everywhere back then. Ancient Greeks wrestled and boxed in them.

HOLLY: Called them *palaestrae.* Singular: *palaestra.*

LAUREL: After Palaestra, the goddess who invented wrestling.

HOLLY: Hear that, boys? The *goddess* of wrestling.

LAUREL: Girl power!

Holly: They wrestled naked.

Laurel: So no place to hide weapons.

Holly: Palaestra ruled the ring.

Laurel: Like we rule the court.

Holly: Victors 20, Opponents 0. Can I get an *Oh, yeah!*?

Laurel: Oh, yeah! Know who I'd like to take on?

Holly: I know who *I'd* like to take on.

Laurel and Holly: The Hunters.

Holly: Check it, newbies. When the Hunters are at camp, we play capture the flag.

Laurel: Hunters 56, Half-Blood 0. Unacceptable result.

Holly: So I'm hiding the flags the next time they show.

Laurel: Can't play capture the flag without flags to capture!

Holly: Then we'll throw down a volleyball challenge.

Laurel: Victors versus Hunters. Two of them against the two of us.

Holly: Those Hunters? They'll look like frightened prey.

Laurel: Deer looking down the wrong end of an arrow.

Holly: Mixed-green salad looking down the wrong end of a fork.

Laurel: What?

Holly: I'm going vegetarian.

Laurel: Hey, me too.

Holly: Since when?

Laurel: Since before you decided to.

Holly: I decided it first!

Laurel: Did not.

Holly: Did too.

Laurel: This conversation is over.

Holly: It's over when I say it's over!

Laurel and Holly: It's over!

TINKERING

THE FORGE

Brought to you by Pete the Palikos

So you're taking a walk in the wild, minding your own business, when – *WHAM!* – a chunk of Celestial bronze falls from the sky and almost kills you. What do you do now? I'll tell you what: you bring that bronze on down to the hottest place in camp – the forge! Cabin Nine campers will jump at the chance to hammer the mystical metal into a weapon, a shield, armour or even – wink, wink – a helmet! While there, you might catch a glimpse of everyone's favourite Cyclops, Tyson. And maybe you can get the Hephaestus kids to ask their dad to watch where he tosses his scraps next time.

THE ARTS AND CRAFTS CENTRE

Brought to you by Pete the Palikos

Creative juices flow freely in this airy studio. It's a favourite place of Athena's children, who come to sculpt, paint, weave and do ceramics, but anyone is welcome to embrace their artistic side here (also their artistic front and top, but please refrain from embracing bottoms). Skeins of naturally dyed yarn, easels with stretched canvases, blocks of marble and clay, and all the tools and paints you could ask for await!

BUNKER NINE

Brought to you by Pete the Palikos

This cavernous workshop lies underground, nestled deep in the woods at the foot of the western hills. Bunker Nine was sealed following the first demigod civil war and eventually lost to memory. For more than one hundred and fifty years, it sat like a time capsule waiting to be discovered. But now, thanks to the fiery touch of Leo Valdez, its secrets and mechanical supplies are within reach. Are you curious enough to venture in?

NUMBER 130 IN BUNKER NINE

by Nyssa Barrera

Bunker Nine is an amazing place. But if you're ever there steer clear of the shadowy corner way in back. Something bad sits there. If you do decide to look, take my advice: don't touch it. Think I'm kidding? Read on.

Late one afternoon, Connor Stoll, Sherman Yang, Valentina Diaz, Paolo Montes, Butch Walker and I were hanging out on the beach when talk turned to camp curses.

'Remember the rhyming-couplet curse Apollo cabin threw that time?' Butch asked. ' "I'm coming in your direction / So get ready for cabin inspection!" '

Valentina giggled. 'My cabin did one years ago called the sweetie curse. Anyone with a secret crush was compelled to call the object of their affection "sweetie".' She glanced at Paolo from under her lashes. 'I wonder what would happen if I hurled that curse now?'

Paolo beamed uncomprehendingly.

Sherman nudged my shoulder. 'What about you, Nyssa? Got any good curse stories?'

I shifted uncomfortably. 'Just one.'

'Well? Let's hear it.'

'I can't. It's more something I would have to *show.*'

I wanted to drop the subject, but they wouldn't let it go. They just kept cajoling me until finally I said, 'All right. Fine. Wait here.'

I ran back to my cabin and retrieved an old book from my storage locker. The book's coal-black leather cover had orange lettering stamped into it, and a small keyhole padlock kept it closed. Reluctantly, I brought it back to the beach. Valentina squealed when she saw it.

'That's a vintage diary, isn't it?' she asked. 'They sold them in the camp store back in the fifties!'

'This one is from the forties,' I corrected. 'It belonged to Heloise, one of my siblings. I found it stashed behind a false panel under my bunk.'

Valentina rubbed her hands eagerly. 'OMG, I *love* reading other people's diaries! Uh, not that I would ever do that without permission, of course,' she added hurriedly.

'So what does Heloise's diary have to do with curses?' Sherman asked.

'Everything,' I said grimly. 'Listen.'

June 10, 1948

Diary:

Back at camp. This summer's project: a race car that runs on Greek fire.

June 13, 1948

Diary:

Sketches complete. Materials gathered. Construction starts tomorrow.

June 16, 1948

Diary:

Outraged. Caught a son of Aphrodite poking around my stuff. Claims he's a car fanatic and came to check out my wheels. Lies, most likely.

June 17, 1948

Diary:

The boy came back. He asked questions about my car. Smart questions. Might have misjudged him.

June 19, 1948

Dear Diary:

James has blond hair and sky-blue eyes. Girls are in love with him. The naiads, too. They dragged him into the lake today and almost drowned him. Ridiculous.

June 20, 1948

Dear Diary:

James brought me a jar of Greek fire at lunch today. All the other girls stared at me.

June 22, 1948

Dear Diary:

The car is finished. I put in butter-yellow leather seats and painted it sky blue.

June 26, 1948

Dear Diary:

First test-drive successful! James wanted to do it, but I wouldn't let him. If anything bad happened, I'd want it to happen to me . . .

June 28, 1948

Dearest Diary:

James says he wants to be an actor some day, but if that

doesn't work out maybe he'll be a race-car driver – but only if I design his car. I think he was joking.

June 30, 1948

Dearest Diary:

The second test-drive was even better. I let James put in the Greek fire. A little must have leaked out because when our hands touched, my fingers burned.

July 2, 1948

Dearest Diary:

James drove the car around the chariot track today. The other girls watched him. He hugged me after and said the car's engine purrs like a kitten.

July 2, 1948 (midnight)

Dearest Diary:

I'm purring too.

July 3, 1948

Dearest Diary:

Tomorrow night there will be fireworks on the beach. I'll help set them up. Then I'll look for James.

July 4, 1948

Diary:

I found him. With an Ares girl.

July 5, 1948

Diary:

The car exploded in the middle of the night. I told Chiron it was the Greek fire. I told James I'm not building another one.

July 8, 1948

Diary:

James visits the armoury a lot these days.

July 10, 1948:

Diary:

I have a new project: Harmonia's necklace.

The diary ended there.

I took a deep breath and looked at my friends. They were staring at me with rapt attention.

'Harmonia was the daughter of Ares and Aphrodite,' I told them. 'As you probably know, Aphrodite was my dad's wife. When Hephaestus found out about Harmonia . . . well, he wasn't too happy with Aphrodite. He fashioned a cursed item.'

Valentina put her hand to her mouth. 'He *cursed* my mom?'

'Not her – Harmonia. He made a beautiful cursed necklace and gave it to her on her wedding day. The rest of her life was basically misery. Same for anyone who wore the necklace after her.'

Butch frowned. 'So what does Harmonia's story have to do with Heloise and James?'

Valentina rolled her eyes. 'You're so thick! Heloise, daughter of Hephaestus, was in love with James, son of Aphrodite. Then she caught him with a daughter of Ares. The love triangle repeated.'

I nodded. 'And then Heloise started working on a project called Harmonia's necklace.'

'A curse for the boyfriend who jilted her,' Sherman said.

'Yeah.' I showed them a black-and-white photograph of a cute teenage boy in an old-fashioned Camp Half-Blood T-shirt, sitting next to a girl who looked like a younger version of Rosie the Riveter. 'James and Heloise in 1948. And this is James in 1955.'

I pulled out a close-up of a twenty-something

man with chiselled features and a sultry expression. 'Anyone recognize him?'

Valentina's jaw dropped. 'It's James Dean!'

'The sausage tycoon?' Butch asked.

'Not *Jimmy* Dean, you idiot. *James* Dean. The actor.' Valentina smoothed her hand over the photo. 'He was a total hottie.'

'Hottie!' Paolo confirmed in a heavy Brazilian accent. '*Rebel. Eden.* Dead young.'

'Right,' I said. 'James Dean rocketed to superstardom in 1955 with two movies, *East of Eden* and *Rebel Without a Cause.*'

'What did Paolo mean by "dead young"?' Connor asked.

I showed them a third photo of James. He was sitting in a sleek silver race car with the number 130 painted on the hood and sides. 'This was taken around September twenty-second, 1955. Nice car, huh? It's a Porsche 550 Spyder.' I laid down one last photo. 'And *this* was taken on September thirtieth.'

They all gasped. The Spyder was a mangled wreck of twisted metal, identifiable only by the number 130.

'James and a friend were driving to Salinas, California, for a race,' I told them. 'They stopped at a roadside store. The accident happened about half an hour later. James was killed in the crash.' I chewed my lip. 'I think Heloise cursed the car when it was at the rest stop. She installed something, enchanted the chassis. I don't know, exactly, but that was her secret project, code-named Harmonia's necklace.'

Sherman frowned. 'Car accidents happen all the time, Nyssa.'

'Yeah, but listen to this: the guy who hit them claims he never saw the car coming. After the crash, parts salvaged from the Spyder were installed in other cars – and *those* cars were in horrible accidents. The wreck itself toppled from a truck bed and crushed a man's leg. A pair of thieves suffered freak injuries while trying to steal the steering wheel and seat covers. A garage housing the Spyder's remains caught fire – but the car itself was untouched. Need I go on?'

'Where's the car now?' Sherman asked.

'It vanished in 1959. No mortal knows where it is.'

'Hang on,' Butch said. '*No mortal?*'

I gazed towards the western hills. 'It's in Bunker Nine. I think my dad hid it there. Or maybe Heloise did, to prevent the curse from hurting any more people.' I looked at them. 'Or to keep it as a trophy of her success.'

So that's the story. Maybe the curse on number 130 has faded. You want to touch that wreck in the shadows and find out, be my guest. Me, I'm steering clear.

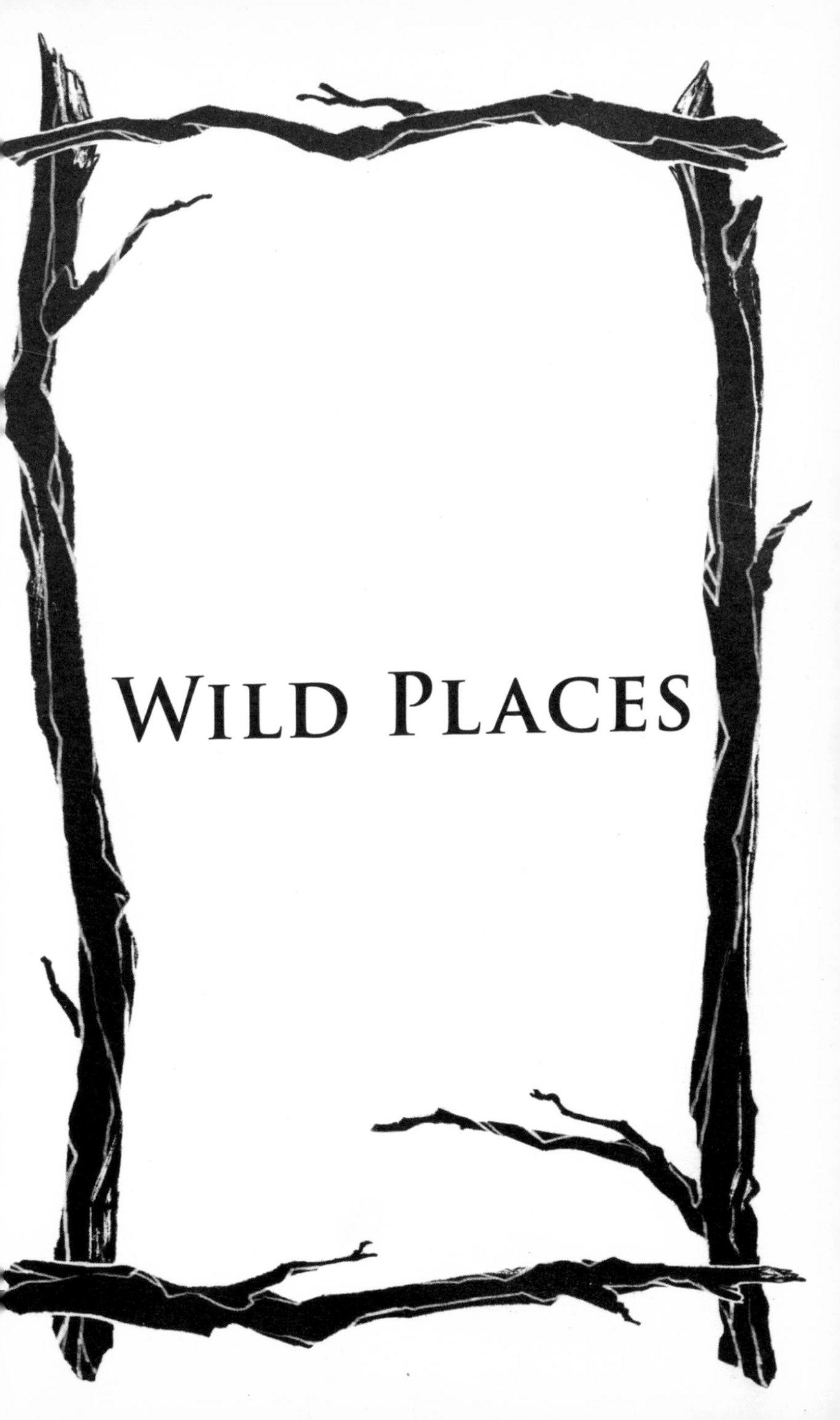

Wild Places

SCENE: The set of a game show. Three campers sit behind a table with dinger bells in front of them. Apollo stands behind a podium. He's dressed as a cheesy game-show host – open shirt, bright gold lamé jacket, skinny black trousers.

APOLLO: Welcome to our first annual Camp Half-Blood quiz show! Please give a warm welcome to our contestants. From Athena cabin . . . Bea Wise! [applause] From Ares cabin . . . Arnold Beefcake! [applause] And representing our cloven-hoofed friends . . . Ferdinand Underwood the satyr! [hoof stomps] Contestants, you know the rules. I ask a question. If you know the answer, ding your bell. Are you ready?

WISE [tapping temple]**:** I think, therefore I am.

BEEFCAKE [flexing]**:** Do your worst!

UNDERWOOD: Um, I ate my bell.

APOLLO: Excellent! Then let's begin. First question: name the serpent I slayed.

[Ding-ding!]

APOLLO: Wise?

WISE: That's not a question.

APOLLO: Sorry, 'That's not a question' is incorrect.

WISE: No, wait, I meant –

[Ding-ding!]

BEEFCAKE: The serpent was Python!

APOLLO: Correct!

BEEFCAKE [showing two thumbs-up]**:** Ayyyyy!

APOLLO: Next question –

UNDERWOOD: So, should I just say *ding-ding* if I know the answer or –?

APOLLO: Who falsely accused me of flaying him alive after a music contest?

UNDERWOOD: Blaa-blaa!

APOLLO: I'm sorry, 'blaa-blaa!' is incorrect. Also, you didn't ring in. The correct answer is Marsyas the satyr.

WISE: Hang on! I knew that! You didn't give me a chance to answer!

APOLLO: He thought he was so great on those stupid twin pipes, but I showed him.

BEEFCAKE: Yeah, you did!

WISE: I thought you were *falsely* accused.

UNDERWOOD: Blaa-blaa!

APOLLO: Final question: do you know what time it is?

[Ding-ding!]

WISE [checks sun's location]**:** Two twen–

APOLLO: It's dancing time! [rips off jacket and shirt and starts hula-hooping] Hit it, boys!

[Satyrs enter flailing ribbon sticks and tootling on reed pipes, and cavort about the sun god]

BEEFCAKE: Oh, yeah! [rips off shirt, twirls it in the air] Now it's a party!

WISE [rubbing temples]**:** I can't believe I studied for this.

FERDINAND: Ding-ding?

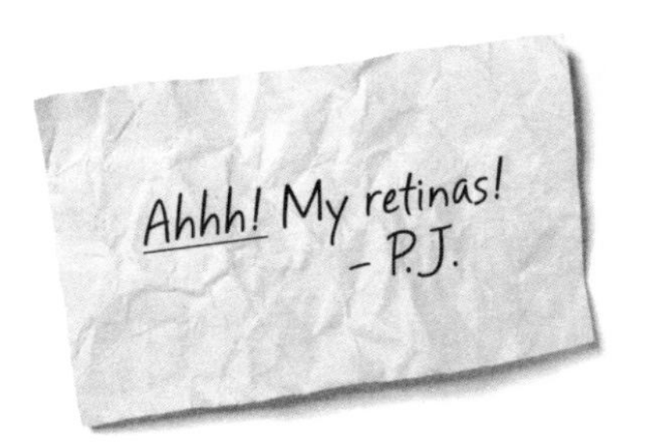

GROVE OF THE COUNCIL OF CLOVEN ELDERS

Brought to you by Pete the Palikos

Scouting around for a place of natural beauty for your next meeting? Consider reserving this idyllic, out-of-the-way clearing! Majestic old-growth trees surround a blanket of soft grass. Leaves rustle in the gentle breezes wafting in from the nearby shore. It's a short hike north of the pegasus stables but worth every step. Iris-message ahead and the forest dryads will arrange for snacks and drinks.

> Note: special permission needed to use the rosebush topiary thrones.

LIVE AND LEARN . . . SO YOU CAN KEEP LIVING

by Woodrow the Satyr

I was honoured when Percy Jackson asked me to tell you about the survival-skills class I teach. Honoured but puzzled, because I teach Reed Pipe Music Composition and Appreciation, not Survival 101.

So I sent paper-aeroplane letters to two satyrs who'd taught the class before, Grover Underwood and Gleeson Hedge, to ask for their advice. Here are their replies:

[Sent on a slightly chewed brown paper bag]

Dear Woodrow,

California is dry. Thanks for asking.

I used the KISS approach – Keep It Simple, Satyr – when I taught the class, because so many students were ADHD. Here, in a nutshell, is my lesson plan. (If you don't have a nutcracker, you can probably borrow one from the dining pavilion dryads.)

Step one: scan your surroundings for immediate threats. Examples: fast-approaching monsters with claws deployed and fangs dripping venom; cavernous pits rimmed with rotten banana peels; clowns (both happy- and sad-faced).

Step two: take inventory. Helpful items to look for: water. Food. Fire. More food.

Step three: stay put and wait for rescue. Note: this last step only works if others are looking for you.

Hope this helps!

Wildly yours,

Grover

[Written on the back of a crayon drawing of a daddy satyr, a mommy wind nymph and a tiny baby kid]

Woodrow,

Surviving is all about beating the odds. Also the evens. Those evens can be sneaky, so *don't take your eyes off them*!

As for the beating, you can't go wrong with a sturdy length of wood. Ash is best – strong, lightweight, makes an excellent *crack* sound when it connects with its target. Stay away from pine. Smells nice, but too sticky. And you never know who might be living inside it.

If you don't have a club handy, try a hoof-kick

to the solar plexus, a horn-stab to the throat and a rump-butt to the gut. Boo-ya!

Coach

I appreciated this sage advice but decided to seek my own technique for survival training. So I did what I often do when contemplating a challenge: I looked to the stars for guidance. That's when it hit me – I could teach demigods to look to the stars for guidance!

Constellations are awesome orientation and navigation tools. They have great historic significance, too, since they're made up of beings and people placed in the heavens by the Greek gods. So it was a win-win concept.

Here's a little taste of my proposed lesson plan:

WHATEVER, MOTHER (OR THE W-M-SHAPED CONSTELLATION)

Cassiopeia, queen of Ethiopia, bragged that she and her daughter, Andromeda, were more beautiful than Poseidon's girls, the Nereids.

'Gods, Mother, embarrass me much?' groaned Andromeda.

The Nereids complained to their dad. As punishment for Cassiopeia's boast, Poseidon sent Cetus the sea monster to wreak havoc on Ethiopia. The only way to end the reign of terror was to sacrifice Andromeda to the beast.

Naturally, Cassiopeia didn't tell her daughter that. Instead, she lured Andromeda to the coast with promises of a lovely spa day by the sea. Once there, she chained her to a rock within easy snacking distance of Cetus.

'Mo-*ther*!' Andromeda was heard to complain over the pounding of the waves. 'These chains clash with my outfit! The salt spray is making my hair frizz! And when is my masseuse getting here?'

'Here he comes now!' Cassiopeia called back as Cetus reared out of the surf and charged the princess. (Note: Grover would have identified Cetus as an 'immediate threat'.)

Seconds before the monster struck, a figure swooped out of the sky. It was the hero Perseus! He drew his sword of diamonds ('Ooo! Shiny!' Andromeda was heard to say over Cetus's snarls), slew the beast, freed Andromeda, controlled her frizz with smoothing serum and married her. They had nine children, founded the city of Mycenae and lived happily ever after.

When they died, Perseus and Andromeda were turned into constellations. They're so dim, though, that they can be hard to find. Instead, look for Cassiopeia, who was also set in the stars. As pushy in the heavens as she was on Earth, you can't miss her pattern: five bright stars that form a *W* or *M* shape, depending on how you look at it. Find it, and you're on the right track to getting home.

FYI: Mother and daughter constellations are very close to each other. So close, in fact, that if you listen in on a moonless night you can hear Andromeda telling Cassiopeia to 'back off and give her some space already'.

Bear With Me

Zeus was sneaking around behind Hera's back – again – with a lovely female named Callisto, who happened to be one of Artemis's Hunters. Why Callisto broke her vow to stay away from men is anyone's guess. Some say Zeus tricked her by disguising himself as Artemis.

Hera found out about Zeus's infidelity – again – and with one angry *poof* turned Callisto into a bear, which she then asked Artemis to hunt. Or maybe she asked Arcas, who was Zeus and Callisto's son and a skilled archer. The details are a little murky. Either way, Callisto the bear was staring down the pointy end of a drawn arrow when Zeus finally took notice.

'Hmm. This may be partially my fault,' Zeus confessed as he defused the threat. Callisto reared up on her hind legs, crossed her paws over her hairy chest and gave him the bear version of 'You *think*?'

'Let me make it up to you.' He transformed her into stars and lobbed them into the sky. He did the same for Arcas, figuring the boy would be safe from Hera that way. The stars formed patterns that looked like bears, which is why the Greeks named them the Big Dipper and the Little Dipper.

Ha-ha! Just kidding! The Greeks called them Ursa Major and Ursa Minor, or the Great Bear and the Little Bear. Ursa Major looks like a – well, like a big water dipper, actually, with a bent handle and a wide-mouthed bowl. Ursa Minor is a smaller version of a dipper with a handle that bends up instead of down.

FYI: rumour has it that Zeus and Callisto secretly hang out when he's in his Roman form. He hides in the planet Jupiter – or maybe he becomes the planet Jupiter – and she revolves around him in the nearby moon named after her. Watch for a supernova in that quadrant of the sky when Hera discovers their trysts.

Look to the Stars for Guidance

So, how do these stories help if you're lost? If you can pick out Ursa Major, Ursa Minor and Cassiopeia in the night sky, you can find north. The three constellations are bunched up around Polaris, the one fixed star in the sky. Find the constellations, and you can find Polaris. Find Polaris, and you've found north. Find north, and you can figure out where east, west and south are. And then you're as good as home!

Note: when I shared my lesson plan with Grover, he pointed out that this method of navigation only works if you know in which direction your home lies. Also, it has proven to be less effective during daylight hours. Oh, well. It's a start.

THE PEGASUS STABLES

Brought to you by Pete the Palikos

Winged horses need a place to call home, too, and Camp Half-Blood is delighted that some have made theirs here. Cleaning the stables might not be much fun, but the flights more than make up for it. So if you fancy a horse-powered swoop through the sky, stop by and meet the herd – and be sure to bring doughnuts!

THE MYRMEKES' LAIR

Brought to you by Pete the Palikos

This site should come with a warning sign: KEEP OUT! If ever you find yourself near the monstrous anthill, be sure to ditch any shiny metal you might have on your person. The giant ants find it irresistible. What they *don't* like are certain waterways. The Zephyros Creek runs between the main campgrounds and the ants' lair, which is probably why they haven't invaded – though the queen ant might just do a fly-by sometime. If they ever decide to cross Long Island Sound, however, New York City could be in for a world of hurt.

THE GEYSERS

Brought to you by Pete the Palikos

Come to a land apart . . . a land of misty magic and moist tropical breezes, where delightful humidity thickens the air and kisses your skin until it glows. You'll know you're near when sweat trickles down your back, dampens your hair and weighs down your clothes. Once here, give voice to your offering to the geyser gods – a poem, a song or a joke told with spot-on comedic timing. Then thrill to the *whoosh* of water from the amazing twin gushing geysers! Bow in the presence of the powerful palikoi! And be sure to fill out the customer satisfaction survey before you leave!

WATER, WATER, EVERYWHERE

by Pete the Palikos

Being a god of a local underground water supply, I'm naturally tapped in to the goings-on at Camp Half-Blood. Exploding toilets? Heard about that one. Son of Poseidon claimed in a stream during capture the flag? Got the details courtesy of Zephyros Creek. Underwater kiss? Canoe Lake gushed about it for days afterwards.

Stories like that trickle in to Paulie and me all the time. We've heard stuff that made us flush. I'd tell you more, but I don't want to flood you with information that might bog you down. But pay us a visit sometime if you want.

We'd come to you, but Chiron has banned us from the showers.

THE STRAWBERRY FIELDS

Brought to you by Pete the Palikos

Is there a tastier treat on a hot summer day than a plump, juicy, sun-warmed strawberry? Mouthwateringly delicious, you can't eat just one. Luckily, here at Camp Half-Blood, strawberries are always on the menu – and on the outbound delivery truck!

PICK YOUR OWN

by Miranda Gardiner

Unless you're a child of Demeter or Dionysus, you'll probably overlook the strawberry fields while you're at Camp Half-Blood. I get that. Unlike the combat arena, the climbing wall, Half-Blood Hill and other common areas, the fields are ordinary – well, except for the whole growing-perfect-berries-year-round thing.

It's too bad if you overlook the place, though, because the strawberries play a vital role at camp. They make us money, which pays for a lot of useful stuff here at Camp Half-Blood. Think that complimentary orange T-shirt you're wearing just magically appeared out of nowhere? Not quite.

You might be interested in knowing how the decision to grow strawberries came about. Then again, you might not. Feel free to move on to the next chapter if you're not. Just know you'll be missing out on some truly delicious camp info.

Still with me? Okay, here's how it went down.

Back in ancient times, Camp Half-Blood was

self-sustaining – a bastion of locally grown produce and free-range meat and poultry products. When the camp moved to Long Island, though, the crops and herds didn't come with it. For a long while campers had to make do by hunting, fishing and gathering, Old-World-caveman-style. What we couldn't hunt and gather, we traded for with local farmers, which was okay when Long Island was sparsely populated.

Then New York City ballooned into a megalopolis and urban sprawl oozed onto the island, with communities erupting nearby almost overnight. After the third mortal sighting of teenage demigods running through neighbourhoods with bows and arrows, Chiron decided it was time to make some changes.

He convened the head counsellors of the nine inhabited cabins to discuss the issue. (The Hephaestus kids were on a quest for Celestial bronze, and Zeus's cabin was empty because he'd curtailed his extracurricular activities to appease Hera. The Hunters were on a stopover, though, so Cabin Eight was occupied.)

'We need a way to supply the camp,' Chiron said. 'Any ideas?'

'Yes! We take what we need by force!' bellowed the leader of the Ares cabin.

'Or we could just, you know, steal it,' suggested the Hermes representative.

'No, no!' The son of Apollo whipped out his lyre. 'We should sing for our supper, as did the minstrels of yore!'

'Of your what?' asked the Dionysus counsellor.

'What?'

' "The minstrels of *your*," ' the Dionysus girl said impatiently. 'Of your *what*?'

A representative of the visiting Hunters intervened. 'Not *your*. *Yore*.'

The Dionysus girl gave up.

'This is getting us nowhere.' The daughter of Athena stood. 'Chiron, the camp needs a steady source of income.'

'Agreed,' Chiron said. 'Suggestions?'

'One.' She rested her fingertips on the table and surveyed the others with great solemnity. 'We will sell something that people will buy in massive quantities.'

'Wine!' called the Dionysus girl.

'Weapons!' yelled the Ares boy.

'Vocal arrangements in four-part harmony!' sang out the Apollo counsellor.

'Food.'

All eyes turned to the Demeter boy who had

spoken. He shrugged. 'People always need food. Big city like New York, lots of people – lots of customers.'

Chiron stroked his beard. 'I like it. But what kind of food?'

That wasn't an easy question to answer. The Athena and Dionysus cabins wanted to sell food associated with their godly parents: olives and olive oil in honour of Athena; and grapes, grape juice, grape jelly and wine (again) for Dionysus. The Hermes, Artemis and Ares kids suggested putting their herding, hunting and slicing-and-dicing talents to use and opening a butcher shop. Poseidon's daughter campaigned loudly for a seafood shack that offered 'both Manhattan *and* New England clam chowder'. Apollo's son, still stuck on his original idea, tried to woo the Aphrodite counsellor to his cause by pointing out that music was the food of love. She wasn't buying it – and neither, she said disdainfully, would any self-respecting customer.

The discussion was escalating into an argument when the Demeter head counsellor offered one last suggestion. 'What about this?' He held out a small red object.

'Miniature explosive!' the Ares boy bellowed. 'Duck!'

'It's not an explosive or a duck,' the Demeter boy said. 'It's a berry native to this land. Grows all over the place here.'

The Aphrodite girl wrinkled her nose. 'Excuse me, but *ew*! There are seeds all over the outside! *So* unattractive. And *red*? That colour is *so* overdone, fruit-wise.'

'Yes, but it's tasty,' the Demeter counsellor said. 'I call it a *strawberry*.'

'Why?' the Athena girl wanted to know.

'Because blueberry, raspberry, blackberry and cranberry were taken. Here, try one.' He spilled a handful onto the table.

The other counsellors and Chiron sampled the strawberries. '*Sweeeet*,' drawled the Dionysus counsellor. Even the Aphrodite girl agreed – though she picked off the seeds first.

Chiron asked the Demeter boy to stand. 'It seems we have our product,' he said. 'Will you and your siblings oversee the crop and grow it in abundance?'

The Demeter boy straightened his shoulders and lifted his chin. 'We will make it our sacred duty,' he said, 'though we might ask the satyrs for backup on the reed pipe and the Dionysus kids for an assist now and then.'

The Dionysus counsellor gave him a thumbs-up.

The Apollo boy strummed his lyre for attention. 'Gentle souls, hear my pledge! I will make it *my* sacred duty to name and market our newfound venture.' He strummed another chord, adjusted the tuning and strummed again. 'I will even compose a catchy jingle to advertise our wares throughout the fair streets of New York. Like a plague, this jingle will infect the minds of everyone who hears it. Soon all the world will sing of our product. The jingle shall go a little something like this . . .'

Fortunately, the other counsellors talked him down before he could create a virulent, incurable ear worm. But the Apollo campers *did* do a great job marketing the new product, obviously keeping secret the fact that our divine new food was, in fact, grown by semidivine beings.

And that, newbie demigods, is how the Delphi Strawberry Service came to be.

Hello? You still reading? Hello?

Shoot. I knew I should have worked in a fight scene.

DO I GET TO KEEP THE T-SHIRT?

AND OTHER FAQs

Answered by Percy Jackson, Annabeth Chase and Nico di Angelo

PJ: We're a little limited on time, so let's get right to the questions.

So, do *I get to keep the T-shirt?*

PJ: You do, but since clothes tend to get slashed, burned and bloodied here, you might want to purchase additional ones at the camp store.

AC: Percy!

PJ: What? Oh. Guess that makes life here sound a little dangerous.

NDA: Deadly, even.

AC: Nico!

PJ and NDA: Anna-be-eth!

AC: Idiots.

PJ: You'll be fine here. Probably. It's when you go on a quest that you'll encounter . . . trouble.

A quest? Do I have to go on a quest?

AC: You may not believe it now, because this is all so new to you, but getting picked for a quest is every demigod's dream. It's what we train for. It's what we're born to do.

PJ: You might not get picked right away. I mean, sure, I did – I was here, what, less than a week before I headed out to face death?

AC: You were a special case, Seaweed Brain.

PJ: Aw, you called me special!

NDA: She also called you Seaweed Brain.

'Face death'? Am I going to die?

NDA: I'll take this one. Yes, you will die – some day. When you do, you'll go to live, er, to *exist* in the Underworld.

PJ: Leo didn't.

NDA: Leo cheated death with a potion that he shouldn't have had. Without it, he'd have stayed dead. Like he was *supposed* to.

PJ: Hazel came back too.

NDA: That's totally different! I brought her back on purpose.

PJ: Just saying that not everyone who dies stays dead.

NDA: Next question.

What if I don't like it here? Can I go home?

AC: I've never been homesick. I bet that feeling stinks. But, before you pack your bags for home, ask yourself, who will protect you out there in the mortal world? Who will teach you to use your powers? Who will really understand what it's like to be a demigod?

PJ: You can always Iris-message home. I hear moms in particular like that.

Will my conversations be private, or does Iris stay on the line?

PJ: You know, I never thought about that.

AC: I'm sure Iris hits mute. Plus, these days she's too busy running Rainbow Organic Foods and Lifestyles – her new whole-foods, gluten-free, vegan business – to listen in.

NDA: Gods, I'd rather be stuck in a bronze jar with only pomegranate death-trance seeds again than eat that ROFL stuff.

How long has Camp Half-Blood been here?

PJ: Oh, man, that's a toughie. Some date it to the 1860s –

AC: But George Washington was a demigod, so, if *he* trained here, the American version of the camp could be a hundred years older. Wow, I'm going to have to research that.

NDA: You newcomers could always ask your godly parents, but honestly time is so different for the deities I bet he or she doesn't know, either.

Where was it before? I mean, after Ancient Greece?

PJ: Um . . . Annabeth, you want to take this one?

AC: Well, there was Rome, obviously. After the fall of the empire, the camp kind of moved from country to country, depending on which one was the major power of the time. I'm not sure of the exact locations, actually. You'd have to ask Chiron.

PJ: Congrats, kid, you stumped a daughter of the Wise One!

Last question: will I really get zapped by lightning if I call Zeus's Fist the 'Poop Pile'?

PJ: Only one way to find out!

NDA: Go ahead, kid! I'm sure my dad would love to meet you.

AC: Percy! Nico!

PJ and NDA: Anna-be-eth!

AW, SUMMER'S OVER . . .

by Percy Jackson

Pavement, or the surface of a walkway, comes in many forms. There's your asphalt (pronounced *ass-fault*, not *asp-halt*), your cobblestone, your gravel, your concrete, your –

Ha! Gotcha! Bet you thought you'd lost the ability to see through the Mist, didn't you?

What . . . you mean you weren't fooled?

Meh. Okay, then. Back to being serious.

Outside camp, the days are getting shorter and the nights are getting cooler. Inside, campers are talking about classes they'll be taking back at their mortal schools. Summer's nearly over, and that means Camp Half-Blood will be closing. Right?

Wrong!

Camp Half-Blood remains open all year round for demigods who, for one reason or another, can't or don't want to go home. If you fall into that category, just be sure to inform whoever is in charge – Chiron, Mr D, or maybe some other immortal – that you intend to stay. That way, the cleaning harpies won't eat you. Come to think of it, it might be a good idea to state your intentions in writing . . . just to be safe.

I've never stayed past summer, but I've visited a few times in the off-season. It's pretty nice around here then. Quiet, because only a dozen or so campers stick around. Sometimes the magical borders let in snow – the good, packable kind for making snowballs and snow sculptures. It's more relaxed, too, as if trouble has been put on hold. Even the monsters in the woods seem to calm down. (Whoops, did we forget to tell you about those? Our bad.)

From what I've heard, the off-season is a great time for demigods to work on pet projects. For instance, this winter Malcolm will begin weaving the Polias peplos for the Panathenaia (try saying that ten times fast!). Will and Nico hope to find a way to keep Nico from passing out after he shadow-travels. (Did we forget to tell you what that was? Ask Nico about it sometime. Or have him demonstrate – just be ready to catch him.) I suspect Miranda Gardiner and Sherman Yang will be doing many things together; I won't say more, out of respect for their privacy.

As for me, I'll be back home, eating my mom's blue food, going to school and hanging out with

Annabeth. At least, that's my plan. I'd like to say I'm sticking with it. But, because I'm a demigod, my plans seem to change rather unexpectedly.

You'll find that out soon enough. Because guess what?

You're a demigod too.

And now if you'll excuse me . . . someone's blasting on the conch horn outside. That can't be good . . .

CHB

CAMP HALF-BLOOD
Western Hills
The Northern Woods
Satyrs
Grove of Dodona
Zeus's Fist
Council of Cloven Elders Meeting Grove
Wolves
Bunker 9
Zephyros Creek
Myrmekes' Lair
Maenad Party Area
Geysers
Wreckage of Old Automatons
Longer Drakons
Pegasus Stables
The Southern Woods
To Peach Orchard
Archery Range
Combat Arena
Strawberry Fields
N
W
E
S

LONG ISLAND SOUND
The Beach
The Dunes
Eastern Hills
Climbing Wall
Dining Pavilion
Euros Creek
Canoe Lake
Cabins
Green
Hestia's Hearth
Arts & Crafts
Athena Parthenos
Thalia's Pine & Golden Fleece
Half-Blood Hill
Amphitheatre
Armoury
Cave of the Oracle
Forge
Campfire
Volleyball Court
Strawberry Fields
Big House
Farm Road 3.141
To Montauk, etc.

About the Campers (in Order of Appearance)

Percy Jackson – son of Poseidon, god of the sea, and Sally Jackson. Black hair, sea-green eyes, wiry build. Can control water.

Chiron – immortal centaur. Son of the Titan Kronos and the nymph Philyra. Brown eyes, brown hair and beard, powerful white stallion body. Longtime trainer of demigods and current activities director of Camp Half-Blood.

Annabeth Chase – daughter of Athena, goddess of wisdom and weaving, and Dr Frederick Chase. Blonde hair, grey eyes. Superior strategist, outstanding architect, rescuer of the long-lost Athena Parthenos. Hero.

Connor Stoll – son of Hermes, god of thievery, messages and trickery (mortal parent unknown). Blue eyes, brown hair. Younger brother of Travis Stoll. Current head counsellor of Cabin Eleven. Known for pranks.

Valentina Diaz – daughter of Aphrodite, goddess of love (mortal parent unknown). Very attractive.

Rachel Elizabeth Dare – daughter of Mr and Mrs Dare (both mortals, first names unknown).

Red hair, green eyes. Can see the future. Current Oracle of Delphi.

THALIA GRACE – daughter of Zeus, god of the sky, lightning and thunder, and Beryl Grace. Half sister of Roman demigod Jason Grace. Once a pine tree, now immortal lieutenant of the Hunters of Artemis. Spiky black hair, electric-blue eyes. Extremely powerful, but afraid of heights. Hero.

LEO VALDEZ – son of Hephaestus, god of forges, fire and metalwork, and Esperanza Valdez. Brown eyes, black hair, short stature, fidgety. Can summon fire. Hero.

MALCOLM PACE – son of Athena, goddess of wisdom and weaving (mortal parent unknown). Grey eyes, blond hair. Substitutes as head counsellor of Cabin Six when Annabeth Chase is off campus.

ELLIS WAKEFIELD – son of Ares, god of war (mortal parent unknown). Muscular.

LAUREL AND HOLLY VICTOR – twin daughters of Nike, goddess of victory (mortal parent unknown). Competitive and athletic. Dark hair.

NYSSA BARRERA – daughter of Hephaestus, god of forges, fire and metalwork (mortal parent unknown). Brown hair. Shares duties as head counsellor of Cabin Nine with Jake Mason.

WOODROW – satyr (half goat, half man). Instructor at Camp Half-Blood.

PETE – a palikos, god of geysers. Off-white muddy complexion, foamy hair, milky eyes. His bottom half is steam; his top half is that of a muscular humanoid.

MIRANDA GARDINER – daughter of Demeter, goddess of agriculture (mortal parent unknown). Green eyes. Shares duties as head counsellor of Cabin Four with half sister Katie Gardner.

NICO DI ANGELO – son of Hades, god of the Underworld, and Maria di Angelo. Black hair, black eyes, pale skin. Very powerful. Travels regularly between camp and the Underworld. First Greek demigod to learn of Camp Jupiter.

Also mentioned:

FREDERICK CHASE – Annabeth Chase's mortal father.

JULIA FEINGOLD – daughter of Hermes, god of thieves and messengers.

HARLEY – son of Hephaestus, god of forges.

THE HUNTERS OF ARTEMIS – girls who pledged themselves to Artemis, goddess of the hunt, and promised to remain celibate. Granted immortality.

SALLY JACKSON – Percy Jackson's mortal mother.

CLARISSE LA RUE – daughter of Ares, god of war.

PAOLO MONTES – son of Hebe, goddess of youth.

BILLIE NG – daughter of Demeter, goddess of agriculture.

BUTCH WALKER – son of Iris, goddess of rainbows.

SHERMAN YANG – son of Ares, god of war.

And finally the star of the show, an immortal who shines as bright as the sun because he *is* the sun, a god who needs no introduction, please give it up for . . . Apollo!

Glossary

Achilles – the best fighter of the Greeks who besieged Troy in the Trojan War; extraordinarily strong, courageous, and loyal, he had only one weak spot: his heel

Aeneas – a Trojan hero, the son of Aphrodite and a favourite of Apollo; became king of the Trojan people

amphora (**amphorae**, pl.) – a tall ceramic jar

Andromeda – the daughter of the Ethiopian king, Cepheus, and his wife, Cassiopeia; after Cassiopeia bragged that her daughter was more beautiful than the Nereids, Poseidon sent a sea monster, Cetus, to attack Ethiopia; Perseus saved Andromeda from the rock she was chained to as a sacrifice

Aphrodite – the Greek goddess of love and beauty; she was married to Hephaestus, but she loved Ares, the god of war

Apollo – the Greek god of the sun, prophecy, music, and healing; the son of Zeus and Leto, and the twin of Artemis

Arcas – the son of Zeus and Callisto, a nymph follower of Artemis; Zeus disguised himself as

Artemis in order to seduce Callisto; after Hera became jealous and transformed Callisto into a bear, Zeus hid their son, Arcas, in an area of Greece later called Arcadia

ARES – the Greek god of war; the son of Zeus and Hera, and half brother to Athena

ARGONAUTS – a band of heroes who sailed with Jason on the *Argo*, in search of the Golden Fleece

ARGUS – a hundred-eyed giant sent by Hera to guard a nymph named Io

ARTEMIS – the Greek goddess of the hunt and the moon; the daughter of Zeus and Leto, and the twin of Apollo

ASCLEPIUS – the Greek god of medicine; son of Apollo; his temple was the healing centre of Ancient Greece

ATALANTA – a Greek hero; the daughter of King Iasus, who left her on a mountaintop to die because he wanted a son; she grew up in the wilderness and eventually became one of Artemis's Hunters; she sailed with the Argonauts as the only woman among them

ATHENA – the Greek goddess of wisdom

ATHENA PARTHENOS – a giant statue of Athena; the most famous Greek statue of all time

ATHENA POLIAS – an olive-wood, life-size statue of Athena Polias ('of the city') that was located in the temple to Athena at the Acropolis of Athens, Greece

CALLISTO – a nymph who had a son with Zeus and was transformed into a bear by the jealous Hera; Zeus later placed her into the sky as the constellation Ursa Major, or 'the Great Bear'

CASSIOPEIA – wife of the Ethiopian king Cepheus, and mother of Andromeda; she angered Poseidon when she claimed that Andromeda was more beautiful than the Nereids

CELESTIAL BRONZE – a rare metal deadly to monsters

CENTAUR – a race of creatures that is half human, half horse

CETUS – the sea monster Poseidon sent to attack Ethiopia as punishment when Cassiopeia boasted that her daughter, Andromeda, was more beautiful than the Nereids; Andromeda was sacrificed to the monster but ultimately saved by Perseus

CHARMSPEAK – a blessing bestowed by Aphrodite on her children that enables them to persuade others with their voices

CHITON – a Greek garment; a sleeveless piece

of linen or wool secured at the shoulders by brooches and at the waist by a belt

CYCLOPS (CYCLOPES, pl.) – a member of a primordial race of giants, each with a single eye in the middle of his or her forehead

DEMETER – the Greek goddess of agriculture; a daughter of the Titans Rhea and Kronos

DIONYSUS – the Greek god of wine and revelry; a son of Zeus; director at Camp Half-Blood

DRAKON – a gigantic yellow-and-green serpent-like monster, with frills around its neck, reptilian eyes and huge talons; it spits poison

DRYADS – tree nymphs

EIDOLON – a possessing spirit

ENCELADUS – a giant created by Gaia to specifically destroy the goddess Athena

GAIA – the Greek earth goddess; mother of Titans, giants, Cyclopes and other monsters

GOLDEN FLEECE – this hide from a gold-haired winged ram was a symbol of authority and kingship; it was guarded by a dragon and fire-breathing bulls; Jason was tasked with obtaining it, resulting in an epic quest

GREEK FIRE – an incendiary weapon used in naval battles because it can continue burning in water

GROVE OF DODONA – the site of the oldest Greek Oracle, second only to the Oracle of Delphi; the rustling of trees in the grove provided answers to priests and priestesses who journeyed to the site

HADES – the Greek god of death and riches; ruler of the Underworld

HARPY – a winged female creature that snatches things

HEBE – the Greek goddess of youth; daughter of Zeus and Hera

HECATE – goddess of magic and crossroads; controls the Mist

HEPHAESTUS – the Greek god of fire and crafts and of blacksmiths; the son of Zeus and Hera, and married to Aphrodite

HERA – the Greek goddess of marriage; Zeus's wife and sister

HERMES – the Greek god of travellers; guide to the spirits of the dead; god of communication

HESTIA – the Greek goddess of the hearth

HIMATION – an outer garment worn by the Ancient Greeks over the left shoulder and under the right

HUNDRED-EYED – Argus was a hundred-eyed giant sent by Hera to guard Io, a nymph with whom Zeus was involved

HUNTERS OF ARTEMIS – a group of maidens loyal to Artemis and gifted with hunting skills and eternal youth as long as they reject romantic love for life

HYPNOS – the Greek god of sleep

IO – a nymph who attracted Zeus's attention and was guarded by a hundred-eyed giant named Argus

IRIS – the Greek goddess of the rainbow, and a messenger of the gods

JASON – a Greek hero; the leader of the Argonauts' expedition in the quest of retrieving the Golden Fleece

KOPIS – a three-foot-long sword with a forward-curving blade

KRONOS – the youngest of the twelve Titans; the son of Ouranos and Gaia; the father of Zeus; he killed his father at his mother's bidding; Titan lord of fate, harvest, justice and time

LABYRINTH – an underground maze originally built on the island of Crete by the craftsman Daedalus to hold the Minotaur

LYRE – a string instrument, similar to a small harp, used in Ancient Greece

MANTICORE – a creature with a human head, a lion's body and a scorpion's tail

MINOTAUR – the half-man, half-bull son of King

Minos of Crete; the Minotaur was kept in the Labyrinth, where he killed people who were sent in; he was finally defeated by Theseus

MIST – a magic force that disguises things from mortals

MOUNT OLYMPUS – home of the Twelve Olympians

MOUNT PELION – a mountain in the southeastern part of Thessaly in central Greece; the homeland of Chiron the centaur, tutor of many Ancient Greek heroes

MYCENAE – the capital city that Perseus and Andromeda founded

MYRMEKE – a giant ant-like creature that poisons and paralyses its prey before eating it; known for protecting various metals, particularly gold

NAIAD – a water nymph

NEMEAN LION – a lion that ravaged the area of Nemea; its fur was impervious to human weapons; slain by Heracles

NEMESIS – the Greek goddess of revenge

NEREIDS – water nymphs

NIKE – the Greek goddess of strength, speed and victory

NYMPH – a female deity who animates nature

OMPHALUS – stone used to mark the centre – or navel – of the world

ORACLE OF DELPHI – a speaker of the prophecies of Apollo

OURANOS – the Greek personification of the sky; father of the Titans

PALAESTRA – the Greek goddess of wrestling

PALIKOI (PALIKOS, sing.) – twin sons of Zeus and Thaleia; the gods of geysers and thermal springs

PANATHENAIA – an ancient religious festival in Athens; the Athenians went in procession to the Acropolis, sacrificed one hundred oxen, and gave offerings, including a richly embroidered cloth, to the goddess Athena in the Parthenon temple

PARTY PONIES – groups of centaurs that are wild and drink root beer; known for attaching boxing gloves to the tips of their arrows and using paintball guns with Celestial bronze dust mixed into the paint

PEGASUS (PEGASI, pl.) – a winged divine horse, sired by Poseidon, in his role as horse-god

PEPLOS – an outer robe or shawl worn by women in Ancient Greece, hanging in loose folds and sometimes drawn over the head

PERSEUS – a Greek hero; one of his many feats of bravery was rescuing Andromeda from the sea monster Cetus

POSEIDON – the Greek god of the sea and of horses; son of the Titans Kronos and Rhea, and brother of Zeus and Hades

PYTHON – a monstrous serpent that Gaia appointed to guard the Oracle at Delphi

RIVER STYX – the river that forms the boundary between earth and the Underworld

SATYR – a Greek forest god, part goat and part man

SHADOW-TRAVEL – a form of transportation that allows creatures of the Underworld and children of Hades to use shadows to leap to any desired place on earth or in the Underworld, although it makes the user extremely fatigued

STROPHION – a garment worn by females in Ancient Greece; a soft band placed underneath the breasts to give them support

TARTARUS – lowest part of the Underworld

TITAN WAR – the epic ten-year battle between the Titans and the Olympians that resulted in the Olympians taking the throne

TITANS – a race of powerful Greek deities, descendants of Gaia and Ouranos, that ruled during the Golden Age and were overthrown by a race of younger gods, the Olympians

TROJAN – of Troy

TROJAN WAR – According to legend, the Trojan War was waged against the city of Troy by the Achaeans (Greeks) after Paris of Troy took Helen from her husband, Menelaus, king of Sparta

TROY – a city situated in modern-day Turkey; site of the Trojan War

TYCHE – the Greek goddess of good fortune; daughter of Hermes and Aphrodite

UNDERWORLD – the kingdom of the dead, where souls go for eternity; ruled by Hades

URSA MAJOR – the Great Bear, the constellation form of Callisto, whom Hera turned into a bear in a fit of jealousy and Zeus made eternal by making her a cluster of stars

URSA MINOR – the Little Bear, the constellation form of Arcas, Zeus's son with Callisto

ZEUS – the Greek god of the sky and the king of the gods

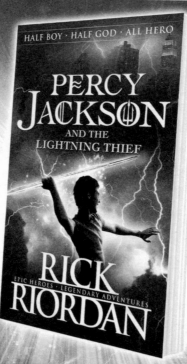

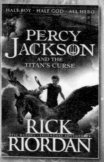

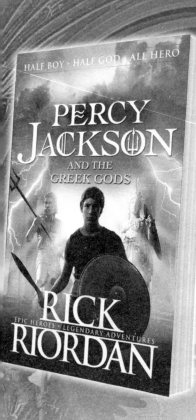

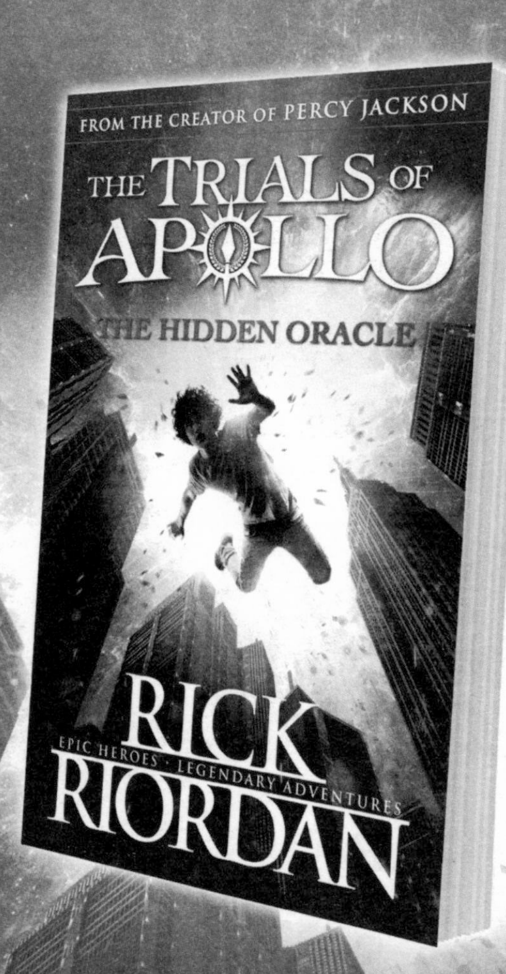
FROM THE CREATOR OF PERCY JACKSON
THE TRIALS OF APOLLO
THE HIDDEN ORACLE
RICK
EPIC HEROES · LEGENDARY ADVENTURES
RIORDAN

A PERILOUS QUEST TO COMPLETE.
I MUST BECOME A GOD AGAIN.

APOLLO'S TRIALS ARE JUST GETTING STARTED . . .

TURN THE PAGE FOR A SNEAK PEEK
AT THE NEXT ADVENTURE!

THE TRIALS OF APOLLO

THE DARK PROPHECY

1

Lester (Apollo)
Still human; thanks for asking
Gods, I hate my life

WHEN OUR DRAGON declared war on Indiana, I knew it was going to be a bad day.

We'd been travelling west for six weeks, and Festus had never shown such hostility towards a state. New Jersey he ignored. Pennsylvania he seemed to enjoy, despite our battle with the Cyclopes of Pittsburgh. Ohio he tolerated, even after our encounter with Potina, the Roman goddess of childhood drinks, who pursued us in the form of a giant red pitcher emblazoned with a smiley face.

Yet, for some reason, Festus decided he did not like Indiana. He landed on the cupola of the Indiana Statehouse, flapped his metallic wings and blew a cone of fire that incinerated the state flag right off the flagpole.

'Whoa, buddy!' Leo Valdez pulled the dragon's

reins. 'We've talked about this. No blowtorching public monuments!'

Behind him on the dragon's spine, Calypso gripped Festus's scales for balance. 'Could we please get to the ground? Gently this time?'

For a formerly immortal sorceress who once controlled air spirits, Calypso was not a fan of flying. Cold wind blew her chestnut hair into my face, making me blink and spit.

That's right, dear reader.

I, the most important passenger, the youth who had once been the glorious god Apollo, was forced to sit in the back of the dragon. Oh, the indignities I had suffered since Zeus stripped me of my divine powers! It wasn't enough that I was now a sixteen-year-old mortal with the ghastly alias Lester Papadopoulos. It wasn't enough that I had to toil upon the earth doing (ugh) heroic quests until I could find a way back into my father's good graces, or that I had a case of acne that simply would not respond to over-the-counter zit medicine. Despite my New York State junior driver's licence, Leo Valdez didn't trust me to operate his aerial bronze steed!

Festus's claws scrabbled for a hold on the green copper dome, which was much too small for a dragon his size. I had a flashback to the time I installed a life-size statue of the muse Calliope on my sun chariot and the extra weight of the hood ornament made me nosedive into China and create the Gobi Desert.

Leo glanced back, his face streaked with soot. 'Apollo, you sense anything?'

'Why is it my job to sense things? Just because I used to be a god of prophecy –'

'You're the one who's been having visions,' Calypso reminded me. 'You said your friend Meg would be here.'

Just hearing Meg's name gave me a twinge of pain. 'That doesn't mean I can pinpoint her location with my mind! Zeus has revoked my access to GPS!'

'GPS?' Calypso asked.

'Godly positioning system.'

'That's not a real thing!'

'Guys, cool it.' Leo patted the dragon's neck. 'Apollo, just try, will you? Does this look like the city you dreamed about or not?'

I scanned the horizon.

Indiana was flat country – highways crisscrossing scrubby brown plains, shadows of winter clouds floating above urban sprawl. Around us rose a meagre cluster of downtown high-rises – stacks of stone and glass like layered wedges of black and white liquorice. (Not the yummy kind of liquorice, either; the nasty variety that sits for aeons in your stepmother's candy bowl on the coffee table. And no, Hera, why would I be talking about you?)

After falling to earth in New York City, I found Indianapolis desolate and uninspiring, as if one proper New York neighbourhood – Midtown, perhaps – had been stretched out to encompass the entire area of Manhattan, then relieved of two-thirds of its population and vigorously power-washed.

I could think of no reason why an evil triumvirate of Ancient Roman emperors would take interest in such a location. Nor could I imagine why Meg McCaffrey would be sent here to capture me. Yet my visions had been clear. I had seen this skyline. I had heard my old enemy Nero give orders to Meg: Go west. Capture Apollo before he can find the next Oracle. If you cannot bring him to me alive, kill him.

The truly sad thing about this? Meg was one of my better friends. She also happened to be my demigod master, thanks to Zeus's twisted sense of humour. As long as I remained mortal, Meg could order me to do anything, even kill myself . . . No. Better not to think of such possibilities.

I shifted in my metal seat. After so many weeks of travel, I was tired and saddle-sore. I wanted to find a safe place to rest. This was not such a city. Something about the landscape below made me as restless as Festus.

Alas, I was sure this was where we were meant to be. Despite the danger, if I had a chance of seeing Meg McCaffrey again, of prising her away from her villainous stepfather's grasp, I had to try.

'This is the spot,' I said. 'Before this dome collapses under us, I suggest we get to the ground.'

Calypso grumbled in ancient Minoan, 'I already said that.'

'Well, excuse me, sorceress!' I replied in the same language. 'Perhaps if you had helpful visions, I'd listen to you more often!'

Calypso called me a few names that reminded me how colourful the Minoan language had been before it went extinct.

'Hey, you two,' Leo said. 'No ancient dialects. Spanish or English, please. Or Machine.'

Festus creaked in agreement.

'It's okay, boy,' Leo said. 'I'm sure they didn't mean to exclude us. Now let's fly down to street level, huh?'

Festus's ruby eyes glowed. His metal teeth spun like drill bits. I imagined him thinking, Illinois is sounding pretty good right about now.

But he flapped his wings and leaped from the dome. We hurtled downward, landing in front of the statehouse with enough force to crack the sidewalk. My eyeballs jiggled like water balloons.

Festus whipped his head from side to side, steam curling from his nostrils.

I saw no immediate threats. Cars drove leisurely down West Washington Street. Pedestrians strolled by: a middle-aged woman in a flowery dress, a heavy-set policeman carrying a paper coffee cup labelled CAFÉ PATACHOU, a clean-cut man in a blue seersucker suit.

The man in blue waved politely as he passed. 'Morning.'

''Sup, dude,' Leo called.

Calypso tilted her head. 'Why was he so friendly? Does he not see that we're sitting atop a fifty-ton metal dragon?'

Leo grinned. 'It's the Mist, babe – messes with mortal eyes. Makes monsters look like stray dogs. Makes swords look like umbrellas. Makes me look even more handsome than usual!'

Calypso jabbed her thumbs into Leo's kidneys.

'Ow!' he complained.

'I know what the Mist is, Leonidas –'

'Hey, I told you never to call me that.'

'– but the Mist must be very strong here if it can hide a monster of Festus's size at such close range. Apollo, don't you find that a little odd?'

I studied the passing pedestrians.

True, I had seen places where the Mist was

particularly heavy. At Troy, the sky above the battlefield had been so thick with gods you couldn't turn your chariot without running into another deity, yet the Trojans and Greeks saw only hints of our presence. At Three Mile Island in 1979, the mortals somehow failed to realize that their partial nuclear meltdown was caused by an epic chainsaw fight between Ares and Hephaestus. (As I recall, Hephaestus had insulted Ares's bell-bottom jeans.)

Still, I did not think heavy Mist was the problem here. Something about these locals bothered me. Their faces were too placid. Their dazed smiles reminded me of ancient Athenians just before the Dionysus Festival – everyone in a good mood, distracted, thinking about the drunken riots and debauchery to come.

'We should get out of the public eye,' I suggested. 'Perhaps –'

Festus stumbled, shaking like a wet dog. From inside his chest came a noise like a loose bicycle chain.

'Aw, not again,' Leo said. 'Everybody off!'

Calypso and I quickly dismounted.

Leo ran in front of Festus and held out his arms in a classic dragon-wrangler's stance. 'Hey, buddy, it's fine! I'm just going to switch you off for a while, okay? A little downtime to –'

Festus projectile-vomited a column of flames that engulfed Leo. Fortunately, Valdez was fireproof. His clothes were not. From what Leo had told me, he could generally prevent his outfits from burning up simply by concentrating. If he were caught by surprise, however, it didn't always work.

When the flames dissipated, Leo stood before us wearing nothing but his asbestos boxer shorts, his magical tool belt and a pair of smoking, partially melted sneakers.

'Dang it!' he complained. 'Festus, it's cold out here!'

The dragon stumbled. Leo lunged and flipped the lever behind the dragon's left foreleg. Festus began to collapse. His wings, limbs, neck and tail contracted into his body, his bronze plates overlapping and folding inward. In a matter of seconds, our robotic friend had been reduced to a large bronze suitcase.

That should have been physically impossible, of course, but like any decent god, demigod or engineer, Leo Valdez refused to be stopped by the laws of physics.

He scowled at his new piece of luggage. 'Man . . . I thought I fixed his gyro-capacitor. Guess we're stuck here until I can find a machine shop.'

Calypso grimaced. Her pink ski jacket glistened with condensation from our flight through the clouds. 'And if we find such a shop how long will it take to repair Festus?'

Leo shrugged. 'Twelve hours? Fifteen?' He pushed a button on the side of the suitcase. A handle popped up. 'Also, if we see a men's clothing store, that might be good.'

I imagined walking into a T.K. Maxx, Leo in boxer shorts and melted sneakers, rolling a bronze suitcase behind him. I did not relish the idea.

Then, from the direction of the sidewalk, a voice called, 'Hello!'

The woman in the flowery dress had returned. At least she looked like the same woman. Either that or lots of ladies in Indianapolis wore purple-and-yellow honeysuckle-pattern dresses and had 1950s bouffant hairstyles.

She smiled vacantly. 'Beautiful morning!'

It was in fact a miserable morning – cold and cloudy with a smell of impending snow – but I felt it would be rude to ignore her completely.

I gave her a little parade wave – the sort of gesture I used to give my worshippers when they came to grovel at my altar. To me, the message was clear enough: I see you, puny mortal; now run along. The gods are talking.

The woman did not take the hint. She strolled forward and planted herself in front of us. She wasn't particularly large, but something about her proportions seemed off. Her shoulders were too wide for her head. Her chest and belly protruded in a lumpy mass, as if she'd stuffed a sack of mangos down the front of her dress. With her spindly arms and legs, she reminded me of some sort of giant beetle. If she ever tipped over, I doubted she could easily get back up.

'Oh my!' She gripped her purse with both hands. 'Aren't you children cute!'

Her lipstick and eye shadow were both a violent shade of purple. I wondered if she was getting enough oxygen to her brain.

'Madam,' I said, 'we are not children.' I could have added that I was over four thousand years old, and Calypso was even older, but I decided not to get into that. 'Now, if you'll excuse us, we have a suitcase to repair and my friend is in dire need of a pair of jeans.'

I tried to step around her. She blocked my path.

'You can't go yet, dear! We haven't welcomed you to Indiana!' From her purse, she drew a smartphone. The screen glowed as if a call were already in progress.

'It's him, all right,' she said into the phone. 'Everybody, come on over. Apollo is here!'

My lungs shrivelled in my chest.

In the old days, I would have expected to be recognized as soon as I arrived in a town. Of course the locals would rush to welcome me. They would sing and dance and throw flowers. They would immediately begin constructing a new temple.

But as Lester Papadopoulos I did not warrant such treatment. I looked nothing like my former glorious self. The idea that the Indianans might recognize me despite my tangled hair, acne and flab was both insulting and terrifying. What if they erected a statue of me in my present form – a giant golden Lester in the centre of their city? The other gods would never let me hear the end of it!

'Madam,' I said, 'I'm afraid you have mistaken me –'

'Don't be modest!' The woman tossed her phone and purse aside. She grabbed my forearm with the strength of a weightlifter. 'Our master will be delighted to have you in custody. And please call me Nanette.'

Calypso charged. Either she wished to defend me (unlikely), or she was not a fan of the name Nanette. She punched the woman in the face.

This by itself did not surprise me. Having lost her immortal powers, Calypso was in the process of trying to master other skills. So far, she'd failed at swords, polearms, shurikens, whips and improvisational comedy. (I sympathized with her frustration.) Today, she'd decided to try fisticuffs.

What surprised me was the loud CRACK her fist made against Nanette's face – the sound of finger bones breaking.

'Ow!' Calypso stumbled away, clutching her hand.

Nanette's head slid backwards. She released me to try to grab her own face, but it was too late. Her head toppled off her shoulders. It clanged against the tarmac and rolled sideways, the eyes still blinking, the purple lips twitching. Its base was smooth stainless steel. Attached to it were ragged strips of duct tape stuck with hair and bobby pins.

'Holy Hephaestus!' Leo ran to Calypso's side. 'Lady, you broke my girlfriend's hand with your face. What are you, an automaton?'

'No, dear,' said decapitated Nanette. Her muffled voice didn't come from the stainless-steel head on the sidewalk. It emanated from somewhere inside her dress. Just above her collar, where her neck used to be, an outcropping of fine blonde hair was tangled with bobby pins. 'And, I must say, hitting me wasn't very polite.'

Belatedly, I realized the metal head had been a disguise. Just as satyrs covered their hooves with human shoes, this creature passed for mortal by pretending to have a human face. Its voice came from its gut area, which meant . . .

My knees trembled.

'A blemmyae,' I said.

Nanette chuckled. Her bulging midsection writhed under the honeysuckle cloth. She ripped open her blouse – something a polite Midwesterner would never think of doing – and revealed her true face.

Where a woman's brassiere would have been, two enormous bulging eyes blinked at me. From her sternum protruded a large shiny nose. Across her abdomen curled a hideous mouth – glistening orange lips, teeth like a spread of blank white playing cards.

'Yes, dear,' the face said. 'And I'm arresting you in the name of the Triumvirate!'

Up and down West Washington Street, pleasant-looking pedestrians turned and began marching in our direction.

THE ADVENTURE NEVER STOPS . . .

PERCY JACKSON

THE GREEK GODS ARE ALIVE AND KICKING!

They still fall in love with mortals and bear children with immortal blood in their veins. When Percy Jackson learns he's the son of Poseidon, god of the sea, he must travel to Camp Half-Blood – a secret base dedicated to the training of young demigods.

The Percy Jackson series:

PERCY JACKSON AND THE LIGHTNING THIEF
PERCY JACKSON AND THE SEA OF MONSTERS
PERCY JACKSON AND THE TITAN'S CURSE
PERCY JACKSON AND THE BATTLE OF THE LABYRINTH
PERCY JACKSON AND THE LAST OLYMPIAN

THE DEMIGOD FILES
CAMP HALF-BLOOD CONFIDENTIAL

PERCY JACKSON AND THE GREEK GODS
PERCY JACKSON AND THE GREEK HEROES

HEROES OF OLYMPUS

PERCY JACKSON IS BACK!

Percy and his old friends from Camp Half-Blood join forces with new Roman demigods from Camp Jupiter for a deadly new mission: to prevent the all-powerful Earth Mother, Gaia, from awakening from her millennia-long sleep to bring about the end of the world.

The Heroes of Olympus series:

THE LOST HERO
THE SON OF NEPTUNE
THE MARK OF ATHENA
THE HOUSE OF HADES
THE BLOOD OF OLYMPUS

THE DEMIGOD DIARIES

AN OLYMPIAN HAS FALLEN!

The god Apollo has been cast down from Olympus in the body of a teenage boy. With the help of friends like Percy Jackson and familiar faces from Camp Half-Blood, he must complete a series of harrowing trials to save the world from a dangerous new enemy.

The Trials of Apollo series:

THE HIDDEN ORACLE
THE DARK PROPHECY

THE GODS OF EGYPT AWAKEN!

When an explosion shatters the ancient Rosetta Stone and unleashes Set, the Egyptian god of chaos, only Carter and Sadie Kane can save the day. Their quest takes the pair around the globe in a battle against the gods of Ancient Egypt.

The Kane Chronicles series:

THE RED PYRAMID
THE THRONE OF FIRE
THE SERPENT'S SHADOW

THE GODS OF ASGARD ARISE!

After being killed in battle with a fire giant, Magnus Chase finds himself resurrected in Valhalla as one of the chosen warriors of the Norse god Odin. The gods of Asgard are preparing for Ragnarok – the Norse doomsday – and Magnus has a leading role . . .

The Magnus Chase series:

MAGNUS CHASE AND THE SWORD OF SUMMER
MAGNUS CHASE AND THE HAMMER OF THOR

HOTEL VALHALLA: GUIDE TO THE NORSE WORLDS

ABOUT THE AUTHOR

RICK RIORDAN, dubbed 'storyteller of the gods' by *Publishers Weekly*, is the author of five *New York Times* number-one bestselling middle-grade series with millions of copies sold throughout the world: Percy Jackson, the Heroes of Olympus and the Trials of Apollo, based on Greek and Roman mythology; the Kane Chronicles, based on Egyptian mythology; and Magnus Chase, based on Norse mythology. His Greek myth collections, *Percy Jackson and the Greek Gods* and *Percy Jackson and the Greek Heroes*, were *New York Times* number-one bestsellers as well.

Rick lives in Boston, Massachusetts, with his wife and two sons.

Follow him on Twitter @camphalfblood. To learn more about him and his books, visit:

www.rickriordan.co.uk

WALTHAM FOREST LIBRARIES
904 000 00488817